Treasure Malian

Prologue

Ty

It's been a week since Cairo was taken, and I still couldn't believe the shit. Who wanted Skye this bad that they would go to this length to hurt her? I prayed they didn't hurt Cairo, and I knew in my heart we would get him back because I wasn't stopping until we did. I just prayed they didn't hurt him. I been in NYC trying to get some information, but no one knew anything.

I pulled up to the Waldorf. I stayed at Skye's crib since I been in the city just in case they called her crib. It was unlikely, but we were running out of options. Before I could get out my truck my phone started vibrating, without looking I answered.

"Yo?"

"I have Cairo." The female voice answered

The voice sounded familiar, but it couldn't be. She wouldn't go this far. I shook my head as the reality began to sink in.

"Ty I don't want to hurt him." She spoke up, forcing me to realize that this was real. This shit is really happening.

"Why?" I couldn't bring myself to say anything else, why was all I managed to get out.

She began speaking, giving me a million reasons why she was doing this. The shit didn't matter though, once we got Cairo back the rest would be history. As she went on and on, I sat back and thought about the last time I saw her. I never thought my actions that day would come back around and bite me in the ass like this.

After hearing Ariana lost our baby I couldn't kill her. I couldn't stop myself from wrapping my hands around her neck and nearly sucking the life out the bitch either. I stopped when she started to turn blue. As much as I wanted to kill her, I couldn't. It's not like I loved her, but hearing she lost my baby pinched at my heart. I watched as she gained her composure and listened as she pleaded with me. She explained that she lost the baby the night she got shot. I felt guilty and fucked up that she had to deal with the loss on her own. If she would have told me I would have helped her through it the best way I could have, but she was right way too much was going on at the time.

By that point I had lowered my weapon and made up my mind that I wasn't going to kill her. I stepped back away from her as she sat sobbing on the floor. The damage was done, and there was no getting back from the place we found ourselves at that moment. I was sent to end her life but I couldn't do that either.

"Ariana, just get low. I got a homie out in Vegas who could help you start fresh. Skye wants you dead, and you know the type of shit she been on lately she won't stop. I'll send you bread until you can get on your feet but you gotta go. Don't contact your parents for a minute. Let them call Skye worried. If they don't, she will get suspicious. I hate it had to come to this ma, but this is all you're doing. All you had to do was speak up. I'll contact my nigga then get back at you with the details. Don't take anything." I barked, I prayed she followed my instructions, because if not, this shit wouldn't end well for either of us.

She nodded her head frantically while still trying to catch her breath. I said all I could and needed to say. I concealed my weapon and left.

"You stopped sending the money. How the hell was I supposed to live? Get up two million for me and you can have the baby back unharmed." Hearing her asked for ransom brought me back to the current situation at hand.

"Bitch, I should have killed you!"

Chapter One

Ariana

I wasn't going to sit around and listen to Ty threaten me. I know that he took my demand serious because I already went this far. I didn't need to prove anything else for the moment. I pressed end call, and put the phone down beside me. I focused my attention back on screaming Cairo. I guess he sensed that I wasn't his mother because he cried almost nonstop since we got to NY. He barely allowed me to touch him which made it almost impossible for me to feed him. In no way were my intentions to hurt him. I needed results and I knew that having Cairo would guarantee that. All that was left for me to do was figure out how I could receive what I want, return Cairo and keep my life. Until I had a solid plan in place Cairo would stay in my possession. He was my insurance.

I know that he needed to eat and have some uninterrupted sleep but it just wasn't happening with me.

That's when it hit me. I picked up my phone and called the only person in the world that would be able to help me. I tried to drown out Cairo's cries as I listened to the phone ring, hoping that she answered.

"Hello daughter, it's nice of you to finally decide to call me. I just finish talking to Ty. He's such a nice boy." She said as she answered the phone.

I know I was wrong for keeping my mother out of the loop but at the time it was the only card I had to play. I was supposed to be a dead woman and no one would have believed that for a minute if my mother was her normal upbeat self. I had to stay off the grid for a while. I knew Ty would call there asking for me.

"I know mom, I'm sorry about that you know how things have been with Skye, I just been helping her out. Please don't tell Ty you spoke to me. We are still broken up I'm trying to sort through that without him hounding me." I felt bad lying to her but sometimes you had to tell a little white lie to protect a much bigger issue.

"I know. You don't have to worry your momma knows how that go. How is Skye? And who is that crying like that?" She said biting the bait just as I expected her to.

"She's hanging in there mom and that's Cairo. He's here spending some time with his god mom giving Skye a break." I let the lies flow effortlessly hoping that she would believe them.

"That's really nice of you. Please bring him over I haven't even got to see a picture of him." She said with sadness in her tone.

I knew that she was hurt about the way things went down with her and Adriana a few years back causing a rift in their friendship. My mom tried to push up on Skye's dad and Adriana lost it. I mean I couldn't really blame her. Because of that, my mother avoids all things Adriana related which is why I knew taking Cairo to her house wouldn't pose any threats to my plans. She definitely wouldn't be calling Adriana. Skye wouldn't call my mother either since I'm supposed to be dead. Ty isn't dumb enough to reveal his failure he's going handle this situation on his own. That I knew for a fact. He would never want to risk being seen as untrustworthy to Cam or Skye. My plan was fool proof.

"Okay mom, once he settles down I'll bring him by." I replied doing back flips in head.

We spoke for a little while longer before ending the call. I wasn't going to sit around and wait for Cairo to settle because that would never happen. It wasn't like the nights before when he would just cry himself to sleep. I grabbed his bag and picked him up off the bed before heading out to catch a taxi.

I stood in front of the Marriott Hotel located in downtown Brooklyn and flagged down a cab. As I slid into the back seat of the taxi the cool air from the air conditioning hit me and I let out a sigh of relief. The heat was no joke. We were no more than five minutes into the ride when Cairo drifted off to sleep. I completely forgot that Ty mentioned car rides put him to sleep. I would have been used this method to get some peace and quiet. For the duration of the ride I stared out the window thinking about my next move. If you would have ever told me things would be this way between Skye and I, I would have laughed in your face. I shook my head thinking about all the events that occurred this past year.

As the cab came to a stop in front my mother's brownstone I pulled out a twenty dollar bill and handed it to the driver. Usually I was the type to say keep the change but times have changed. That change was much needed for my next meal. I was jobless and Ty wasn't fronting my bill anymore. The cash I did have left I had to stretch until he came through with what I asked for. When he handed me back my change I stuffed it down into the front pocket of my denim Old Navy shorts. As my Chuck Taylors hit the pavement I chuckled to myself at how my life had changed. Although there was nothing funny about it I had to laugh to keep from crying. There I was parading around in Old Navy and Chucks, don't get me wrong there was nothing wrong with either for anyone else; but it just wasn't my style. It was nothing that I was willing to get used to.

I staggered up the steps with a Cairo sleeping over my right shoulder and his bag slung across the left. I rung the door bell and waited patiently for an answer. Moments later my mother opened the door and instantly reached for Cairo, which was definitely a relief.

Once we were inside the house my mother and I sat in the living and caught up. Of course my version of what I had been up to was completely fabricated as I couldn't come out and tell her the truth about what has been going on. We talked for a minute until Cairo woke up, I automatically expected him to go into one of his crying fits but instead he smile at my mother as she cooed over him.

I took that as an opportunity to slip away and call my boo. I hadn't seen him in weeks; receiving his pipe was long overdue. I thought about his immaculate sex game as I walked up out the living room toward the kitchen and called his phone.

"What up Ari?" He spoke as he answered.

I questioned as I sat down at the kitchen table.

"I just got in the crib from visiting my moms and shit. About to chill, nothing major." He retorted.

"I want to see you. Can you come get me from my mother's house?" I asked hoping that he would come.

Text me the address I'll be out there soon." He said. I could hear the smile on his face. He must have had the same plans as I did.

"Okay I can't wait to see you." I said before hanging up the phone.

I looked down at the phone and saw a text pop up from Man.

Yo Ari what up I need to see you shorty.

Completely ignoring his text I texted my boo the address and headed back into the living room to wait on him with my mother and Cairo.

Skye

I lied in bed tossing and turning, racking my brain trying to figure out who had anything to gain from taking Cairo; but I continued to come up short. I sat up and tossed one of my pillows to the floor and let out an exasperated sigh, I was frustrated. It would have been much easier if I knew where he was so I could have put a plan together to get him back. The unknown was killing me. I just wanted my baby. It had been a week, I hadn't had a proper meal, or an adequate amount a sleep and it was beginning to take on toll on me. I hadn't realized how weak I was until I tried to stand to my feet. Feeling as if gravity was pulling me down toward the floor I sat back on the bed.

The knocking at my door grabbed my attention.

"Come in." I called out with an inkling of energy.

"Hey Sis. Come downstairs and eat. I don't want to hear that you're not hungry, you gotta put something in your system." Victoria said in a sincere tone.

I didn't budge. I understood her concern, it was valid; but I didn't care. Until someone in that house understood how it felt to not know where their child was or if their child was okay I didn't want to hear anything. No one knew the pain and void I was feeling. It was worse than not knowing if Cameron would make. Yes, I was hurting during that time; but this was my son. The pain was incomparable.

I watched as Victoria walked toward me taking slow strides. I knew she was being cautious since as of lately I was snapping on everyone. She needed not to worry at that moment because I just didn't have the energy. She took a seat on the bed next to me and draped her arm over my shoulder. Unconsciously I leaned my head against hers and wept.

"I want my son Victoria." I cried out.

She said nothing. There wasn't anything she could say to console me and she knew that. Instead she rubbed my back while I cried causing my tears form a pool on the pillow that rested on my lap. My phone started to ring causing both Victoria and I to stiffen. We stared at each other for a split second before Victoria pulled the charger out of the base of the phone and lifted it from the nightstand.

She glanced down and her shoulders dropped in disappointment.

"It's Ty." She said as she slid her finger across the screen to answer. "Hey babe." She spoke softly into the phone.

She listened attentively before sticking her hand out to give me the phone. I sat still for a moment not really wanting to talk. I owed it to Ty to take his calls regardless of my mood so I reached for the phone and pressed it against my cheek.

"Yes." I said to alert him that I now had the phone.

"Sis, I don't know how to tell you this..." He began to explain but his choice of words sent me into panic mode.

"No Ty! Unless you are telling me you found my son unharmed and is bringing him back to me I don't want to hear it. Anything else would be totally fucking unacceptable!" I barked into the phone. Not meaning to take my frustration and anger out on him. I just couldn't bare bad news about my son.

"Sis hear me out please." Ty spoke in a soothing tone trying to calm me down.

The only thing that calmed me down was not hearing panic in his voice. I knew how much Ty loved Cairo and if he was about to deliver bad news devastation would surely ooze through his tone and it didn't.

"What happened?" I was growing impatient. I needed him to get to the point and get there fast.

"Ariana has him." Ty said after taking a deep breath.

I didn't hear him clearly. I couldn't have.

"Who?" I asked again for reassurance that I had indeed heard him correctly.

"Ari..." He reiterated.

Time froze, or at least it just felt that way. The steady beat of my heart gradually increased in speed as a million and one thoughts rushed through my mind. I wanted to scream and curse Ty out but what good would that have done. I still needed to get my son back.

"I'm on my way." I said as I pressed end on my phone.

"What happened Sis?" Victoria asked.

Having the first real lead since Cairo was taken I felt optimistic. I knew that I would also have to deal with Ty's indiscretion but it had to go on the back burner until Cairo was back safe with me, where he belonged. I stood to my feet and walked over to my closet completely ignoring Victoria's question. I don't know how serious she and Ty had gotten so I wasn't ready to disclose what he told me to her until I had the facts.

"Sis, what happened?" Victoria asked again this time walking up to me as I stood in my closet in search of something to wear.

"I'm going to home." I replied nonchalantly.

"I'm going with you." She said as she turned on her heels and walked out the room.

I knew there was no point in arguing with her. Once Victoria set her mind or doing something that's exactly what she was going to do. I was seeing more similarities between her and Cameron as the days went on.

As I slipped into the True Religion Shorts and True t-shirt I snatched out the closet my mind floated back to Ty. I still could wrap my brain about the thought of him not completing the one thing I desperately needed him to do. A part of me wanted to blame him for Cairo's kidnapping but then again even if Ty didn't do what I asked Ariana took it to another level bringing my son into this shit. He would definitely have to deal with my but at the top of my list was getting my baby back and personally handling Ariana like I should have done from the beginning.

Once I was completely dressed I grabbed the Chanel bag that was sitting on my chaise and quickly browsed through it making sure it held my necessities. Satisfied that everything I needed was in there I set out to find Victoria and get on the first thing smoking back to New York.

Cameron

Vic just finished telling me that Ty called with a lead on Cairo. I was trying to understand why my right hand nigga didn't reach out to me first. In their eyes I was just some handicap ass nigga who wasn't capable of getting shit done and that was pissing me off. Niggas felt like my attitude and how I been acting was unnecessary but none of them knew how this shit felt. None of them knew how useless a nigga felt. I even had to cut my showers short because a nigga couldn't stand for a certain amount of time before feeling like my fucking legs were going to cave in. This shit was frustrating to say the least.

I wanted to hunt and gun down whoever was responsible for taking my son and it was killing me that I couldn't. I felt like less of a man not being able to step up and handle shit. Handling shit has always been my thing. Even before my pops got killed I was the man of the house. I felt like shit and to make matters worse my girl had to be the man. I knew as time passed I was supposed to start feeling better but as my body got better physically, emotionally I was suffering.

"Victoriaaaaa!" I heard Skye call out.

Hearing her voice made me wanna flip the fuck out. Why shit couldn't be the way it was a few months back. Shit was sweet, I had my girl and we were good.

"I'm in the living room sis." Vic shouted back.

"I was looking for you. You ready?" Skye said as she walked into the living room.

"Yea, I was just talking to Cam." Vic said as she stood to leave.

"You not going to tell me where you going? Or tell your mother for that matter." I asked her wondering why she was acting as if I wasn't present.

"I'm going to get my son. Victoria lets go." She said as she turned to leave with Vic on her heels.

I fell back against the couch and felt a silent scream escape my body. Why was this shit happening? My life had really become the commercial for the slogan "when it rains it pours." Shit seemed to be getting worse by the minute and there was nothing a nigga could do.

I stared at the ceiling when a feeling came over me. I haven't been to church in a minute and I wasn't the most religious person but I did believe in god. I probably had no right but I no other option, for the first time in a while I called on god.

"God, I know I'm not the most deserving person to ask for any favors but I pray that you get my girl and my son through this situation and bring them both back home safe. They have nothing to do with this god it's all me please do me this solid and spare them. Amen."

I couldn't deny the fact that after calling on the man upstairs I felt a little weight lift off my shoulder. I didn't deserve any blessings but I knew for sure god had my little man. He was the only one who was completely innocent and just paying for the sins of his parents. Thinking about my son made me tear up. I haven't cried since my father's death but I missed my little man. Shit was killing me. I closed my eyes and thought about his smile and how it was identical to mine. I thought about my boy until I succumbed to exhaustion and dozed off.

Chapter Two

Ty

Delivering that news to Skye was one of the worst things I had to do to date and I've done some fucked up shit. She was family, and the last thing I wanted was for her to hurt. She didn't deserve it she had been through enough that past year. I knew that I could have gotten Cairo back on my own but it's already been too many secrets. Skye deserved to know the minute I found out it was my fault so I owed her that much at least.

I really wasn't ready to face her or Cameron I knew I would have to answer for the shit I did. Just hope shit would be too sour. I knew that all depended on whether or not we got Cairo back, I wasn't too worried about because I had even intention on getting my god son back. I didn't care who had to be bodied Cairo was going to be returned to Skye and Cam I would die making sure that happened.

I called and texted everybody I knew who knew Ariana and felt confident that someone would hit me back with news that would help me find her even better if they would hit me with her exact location. At that point though any bit of information would have been useful. In the meantime it wasn't shit for me to do except wait for Skye to touch down or one of my niggas to get at me whichever came first.

I kicked my feet up on the coffee table just as my phone started ringing. I picked it up off the seat beside me and saw that it was a text from Skye.

Be at JFK at 6:30

I glanced at the time on my Hublot and saw that I had a few hours to burn before I needed to be at the airport. I set the alarm on my phone and turned up the volume before lying back on the couch with my eyes closed. Since Cairo was taken sleep has been the furthest thing on my mind and now that we were a step closer to getting him back I figured I could snatch some Z's until it was go time.

****

The alarmed blared throughout the house awakening me from my power nap and signaling that it was time for me to head to the airport. I stretched before picking up my phone and going through my text messages.

"Fuck!" I yelled in frustration.

Not one text with info on that bitch whereabouts. I knew I needed to be patient but time wasn't on my side. I headed into the bathroom and quickly washed my face and brushed my teeth before dipping out and heading to the airport.

I pulled up to the airport six thirty on the nose and sent Skye a text letting her know I was there and waiting her. *"You take the clothes off my back and I let you, you steal the food right out my mouth and I watch you eat it..."* Hearing Hov's Holy Grail track coming through the car speakers I reached for the volume and turned it up. I didn't really fuck with the nigga Justin Timberlake but the song was fire. It didn't matter what track it was, if it was Hov a nigga fucked with it, that was the Brooklyn nigga in me.

Hov was rapping about having tats and psycho bitches by the time I spotted Skye and Victoria headed toward the car.

"Fuck, I gotta deal with Vic too." I said out loud just as they opened the back doors and climbed in the truck.

"What up ya'll?" I said as I turned the key in the ignition.

"Hey babe." Vic said.

I glanced back as Skye put her ear buds in and sat back with her eyes closed. I knew she was pissed off with me and I couldn't even blame her. Only way I could have even begun to mend our friendship was by getting her son back. I knew until that happened there wouldn't be any talking to her. I let out a sigh as I pulled off and headed back to Skye's crib.

Skye

When we got to my place I wanted to jump right into the search for Cairo and Ariana. I wasn't in the mood to waste any time definitely wasn't going to waste it talking.

"What information you got for me?" I asked Ty as soon as we walked through the door.

I didn't give him the chance to settle in and I didn't care. Fuck how he felt and fuck him being comfortable! If he would have done what was asked of him we wouldn't even be here.

"Nothing, I hit up everybody who would possibly have information or who I knew could get information. Just gotta wait it out now." He said causing me cock my head to the side and stare at him oddly.

"Wait it out? Nah Ty that's not how this is going to work. I'm not about to sit around and wait for people to get back to you with information while this crazy bitch does only god knows what with my son. That's just not going to work form me." I said hoping he understood that I meant I wanted his feet and ears to the street.

"Crazy bitch? Wait I'm so lost. Who has Cairo?" Victoria asked looking back and forth from me to Ty and back to me.

"Care to share Ty." I said walking into the living room.

"Babe…" Ty started to explain.

I just hated when niggas fucked up and thought they would be able to make it better by starting off their excuse with babe. Females weren't dumb; I knew for sure Victoria wasn't.

"Nah don't babe me. Who has my nephew Ty?" She asked again, this time raising her voice.

"Ariana." Ty said in barely a whisper.

The loud thud is what caught my attention; I turned around to Ty rubbing the side of his face and automatically knew the sound I heard was Victoria's fist colliding with his face.

"The fuck you mean a dead bitch has my nephew." She screamed swinging on him again.

I jumped in between them because I didn't want Ty to hit her back. If he did we would have had to kill him before getting Cairo back and I needed his resources.

"Victoria calm down." I said while pushing her back into the foyer and away from Ty.

"No! Ain't no calm down. He was supposed to kill that bitch sis. Now she has my nephew. Ty word to me on my pops grave if we don't get Cairo back I'ma body you." She screamed out a promise.

Ty probably took it as an idle threat but I knew better. She was her father's daughter and her brother's mini me if pushed it would definitely be slow singing and flower bringing for Ty. I continued to try and calm her down but my efforts were in vain as she continued to rant and curse Ty out. I understood because I wanted to do the same exact thing except I knew I had to stay level headed and focused on the most important goal to me, which my getting my baby.

"What, you was fucking that bitch still Ty? Keep it a rack. You had to be fucking her, it's no other reason why you would cross us like this son. I expected so much more from you." Victoria was mad and hurt.

That moment when she broke down in tears I really realized how much feelings she really had for Ty. I think he noticed it too he tried to get closer to console her but I pushed him back.

"Give her space." I said trying to keep a decent distance between them.

"It wasn't like that, I wasn't fucking her Skye. When I went to her crib I had every intention on killing her." He started to explain.

Although it didn't matter I was curious. I really did want to know what in his right mind made him leave that trifling bitch breathing.

"Then why Ty." I asked him.

"It happened so fast Skye I didn't really have the chance to process it. I just reacted. I was ready to send her to meet her maker when she told me the night she got shot she miscarried my baby. I couldn't kill her. I wanted to sis on everything I really did want to body shorty. I just couldn't do it. She lost my seed Skye. On top of that it was my fault, I took her to the club that night she should have been home with you but I had her in the fucking strip club. Vic I swear I ain't have no feelings for Ari, I wasn't fucking her, wasn't thinking about fucking her or nothing. That shit just fucked me up. So I let her go. I told her to get low because next time she wouldn't be lucky. I really didn't think she would turn around and do some crazy shit like this man." As he spoke I stared at him intensely searching for a lie, or one hint of bullshit and there was none.

I didn't sympathize with Ariana because her losing a child shouldn't have drove her to bringing my son in our beef; but no matter how much I wanted to hate Ty in that instant I couldn't. I totally understood. I'm a mother. Yes my son went full term but every day during my pregnancy I worried that stress would take him from me. If those thoughts would have become my reality I wouldn't have been able to go on living so I completely understood and I sympathized with that.

"I'm sorry sis. You know I love Cai as if the little nigga was my own I would never want him in no shit like this. I know it's my fault and I'm ready to do whatever needs to be done to make it right." He proceeded to apologize.

Ty was never one to bullshit so I took his words to heart and for what they meant.

"I forgive you Ty. Believe it or not I understand. My main focus right now is getting my son back that's all. Nothing else matters to me." I said walking away leaving Ty and Victoria in the foyer alone.

I hoped that they wouldn't come to blows but I needed a breather.

Victoria

I understood why Skye wanted to forgive Ty but I wouldn't give in that easy. He better hope that we get my nephew back unharmed that's the only way I would even consider letting him see another day. I stared at him for a minute before he decided to take a step closer to me. I moved back and put up my hand signaling him not to move.

"I have nothing to say to you Ty." I said as I walked around him toward the back of the house where Skye went.

Her door was open so I walked in without knocked. I found her sitting on the chaise in front her window staring out at nothing in particular.

"You okay?" I asked as I took a seat next to her.

"I will be when I get my son. I really hope she doesn't hurt my baby Victoria. Cairo doesn't deserve to be caught up in my mess; I pray god keeps him safe until I can get him back." She spoke softly on the verge of tears.

"We will get him back sis." I said trying to reassure her.

She didn't respond instead she continued to stare off as if I wasn't present. I knew there was nothing I could really say to make her feel any better. I couldn't relate either, I mean yeah I was hurting and wanted my nephew home safe and sound but she was his mother. Her heart had to be on a different level. She wouldn't hurt for long thought. Not if I could help it. I wasn't going to stop until we got the baby back. Nothing would save Ariana from the pain I plan to inflict on her once I get my hands on her. At that moment though, we didn't have any leads on Ariana's whereabouts so all we could do was patiently wait it out. Information would come, and when it did we would be ready.

Chapter Three

Ariana

My baby came and picked me up from my mother's house as promised. I was just thankful that she didn't protest when I asked her to watch Cairo for a few hours. If it was up to me it would have been days before I went back to get him. He just cried too much plus I knew he would be safe with my mother.

"Shorty you hungry?" His smooth voice brought me out of my own head.

I looked up to him and smiled. "Nah babe I'm good for the moment."

Grabbing the remote he sat down on the couch next to me and started flipping through the channels. I leaned over and rested my head on his shoulder and thought back to when we first started kicked it.

When I first met him I wasn't attracted to him in the least bit. It wasn't because he wasn't cute because he was. He had smooth chocolate skin which I absolutely loved, shoulder lengths dreads that were always neat, almond shaped brown eyes that had a hint of mystery behind them and he was built. I just couldn't focus too much on how good looking he was because at that time Ty and I were kicking it hard. I wasn't checking for nobody but him, especially nobody on his own team. Yea I still messed with Man from time to time but that was different. Man and I had history; it wouldn't be easy to give him up. Definitely couldn't do it cold turkey.

Every time I was around him he would be extra friendly and shit but I didn't pay it any attention. I thought he was on some brother sister shit because that how it was with everyone on the team. However, those thoughts changed on the first day he came to the hospital to see me after I got shot.

"How you feeling?" He said as he walked in the room with flowers and a get well soon card.

"I mean I have been better but I'm alive so no complaining about that." I retorted smiling.

"That's good. Where your man?" He asked in reference to Ty.

"You probably would know better than me. I haven't seen him in a few days I guess he been busy." I said looking down trying to avoid eye contact.

I didn't want him to see how hurt I was that Ty wasn't there.

"If you were my girl, I wouldn't leave you alone in here for a minute. These niggas would have had to put me out." He said taking a seat next to my bed and rubbing my hand.

In that moment I knew that all those lingering hugs and flirtatious smiles was because he was feeling me. That also was the first I looked at him in a different light other than a nigga that was down with the team and I actually felt the attraction growing between us. It didn't help that every day after the initial visit he came to see me. He even offered to take me home from the hospital but I had already told Man that he could and I couldn't risk the two of them bumping into each other. The first few days home I tried to reach out to Ty but he wasn't there so I started spending more time with him and Man. I grew tired of kicking it with Man because I figured that he only was around me so much to get info on Cam and Ty. Information that I honestly didn't have at the time, not that I would have gave it up if I did.

We grew closer and once I realized that things with Ty and I weren't going to be the same my baby and I made it official. We had been hanging tough ever since. He knew about the ordeal that went down with me and Ty he even came to visit me in Vegas a few times. He expressed to me that we were in this together. I just hope he feels that way after he finds out that I'm the one that took Cairo.

Chapter Four

Skye

I woke up to the sun peeking through my window. I had no idea that I even fell asleep. I can't deny that the sleep was much needed. I glanced at the cable box and the bright neon numbers read 9:43am. I sat up and bed and took a few deep breaths before swinging my legs over and planting them both on the floor. I stood up and stretched my five foot three inch frame as high as it could go before heading into the bathroom to wash my face and brush my teeth.

I stared in the mirror at my reflection and nearly cringed. It wasn't because I was ugly or had any signs of wear on tear on my exterior but because I felt ugly inside. Somewhere along the way I lost sight of who Skye was. I was warned that this would happen but me thinking I had everything under control continued to do what I wanted. Disregarding the warnings. Now there I was. I knew that if I was going to be able to put my life back in order I needed to start right away. I planned on it; but not until I got my baby boy and Ariana was taking a dirt nap.

I turned on the shower and peeled the previous day clothes off my body before stepping in. The water massage was feeling really good and was much needed. I stood directly under the shower head and allowed the water to beat down on me like the jets in the Jacuzzi tub at Cameron's house that I absolutely loved. I lathered the Dove body wash in my sponge and proceeded to wash my tired body.

After the shower I slipped into a pair of Victoria Secret PINK sweats and a PINK t-shirt. Not really a typical outfit for me but I didn't really care. I didn't have anyone to impress. As I turned the knob on my bedroom door to join Ty and Victoria it hit me. I skipped back over to my bed and took a seat as I unplugged my cell phone from the charger. I scrolled through the phone book in search of the person who I prayed would have the answers that I desperately needed.

As I listened to the phone ring. I felt my heart rate increase as well as the beating of my heart against my chest walls. The moment was intense because I felt like everything was riding on this one phone call. I knew we wouldn't get any leads from anywhere else so this had to be it.

"Good morning" Ari's mother sang into the phone in her everyday chipper voice.

"Morning, its Skye." I sang back. I couldn't allow her to know that something was wrong so I went into actress mode.

"Hey Lovely. Calling to check on your handsome man. He's so precious Skye." She said, with a smile plastered on her face that I could hear radiating through the phone.

He's there? I thought to myself. Was I that lucky?

"Yes, what is my boy doing?" I said playing along. I needed more information.

"He just finished devouring a bottle." She said with a chuckle.

I knew it was true. Cairo was his father's child. The boy could eat.

"Where is Ariana?" I asked walking out on a limb.

"Honestly I have no idea she and Cairo came over yesterday and she was supposed to be heading out for a few hours. She haven't called or anything." She explained.

"Well, I just got back into the city. Can I come pick up my boy I miss him terribly." I said sounding sad. That wasn't an act that. I really did miss my boy and the sooner I got him back the better I would feel.

"Of course. I'm just glad I finally got to see him. I'll start getting his things ready now." She said.

"Okay I'm on my way." I said quickly hanging up the phone.

I didn't have time to waste. I needed to get Cairo before Ariana decided to call her mother or go back to her house. I got up off the bed and headed out the room. Ty and Victoria were sitting in the living room in silence but I didn't have time to deal with them either.

"I'll be back." I shouted over my shoulder as I headed out the front door to catch a taxi.

****

When the cab came to a complete stop in front of Ariana's mothers Brownstown I handed him a fifty dollar bill and told him to keep the meter running. I needed to be in and out so I hoped to god that she had Cairo ready like she said she would. I stepped out of the cab and proceeded up the steps that led to her front door two at a time. I pushed the door bell and shifted my weight to one side as I grew impatient. I hadn't even given her a minute to get to the door; I just didn't have a minute to waste. When Ariana's mom finally opened the door holding Cairo I felt a weight lift off my shoulder. I reached for my baby and thanked god.

"Cairo!" I squealed as I planted kisses all over his face.

"It was such a pleasure having him over. Let me get his bag." She said as she turned to head into the house.

"It's okay. Keep it for when he comes back to visit you. We gotta head out his aunt wants to see him." I said as I back peddled down the steps.

I promised to call her and told her that Cairo would be back soon although that was the furthest thing from the truth. Once I was back within the safety of the Taxi I let out a hard breath and started to search my baby for bruises. There wasn't any and he appeared to be fine. He was smiling that soft welcoming smile that made my heart flutter. I just knew he was just as happy to see me as I was to see him.

"I love you so much Cairo." I professed my love for him as if he could tell me he loved me back. I didn't need to hear it though. I knew he did.

I'm glad I opted to take a taxi it gave me time to bask in the joy of having my baby boy back. I held him close to my heart with a grip that said I never wanted to let him go. I smothered him with kisses the entire ride and before I knew it the taxi was pulling up in front of my building. I handed the driver another fifty dollar bill before hitting the pavement and heading up to my place.

Ty

I was in the kitchen looking for something to eat when I heard what sounded like a baby cooing. I missed Cai like crazy but I knew a nigga wasn't going crazy and starting to hear shit. I looked over at Vic and saw her looking at me we must have been thinking the same thing. Just when I was ready to go investigate the noise Skye came prancing into the kitchen with Cairo in her arms. He was smiling and speaking the language that only he knew fluently just as always. I never felt so good in my life.

"How? I mean where?" I really couldn't get the question out properly but Skye understood.

She explained that something made her want to call Ariana's mother and she did. One thing led to another and here she was with Cairo safe. I guess that mothers intuition shit was real. I could see a little bit of the old Skye resurface but I knew she wouldn't be completely back until Ariana was handled.

"Ty." Skye spoke while taking a seat at the table.

"Yea wassup?" I questioned. I didn't have a clue what she wanted but whatever it was I was going to do it.

"I need you and Cairo on a plane back to Miami. I would have Victoria take him but I know for a fact she not going to want to leave. I just need Cairo somewhere safe. My mother is there, his grandmother, hector, and his father. I know they won't let anything happen to him." She said. Her tone told me she was dead serious but I secretly hoped that she would change her mind.

What would happen if I left them here alone to go after Ari? I learned a while ago that niggas shouldn't really underestimate Skye. If she knew she could get to the bottom of this on her own I had to respect it. Her track record didn't give me any reason not to.

"Aight Sis. I'll take him. What do I tell Cam?" I asked knowing that I needed to prepare to deal with the hundred and one questions my nigga would definitely ask.

"Nothing. Tell him I gave you Cairo and sent you back. It's not the complete story but it's not a lie either. I'll deal with Cameron when I get back to Miami which hopefully will be tonight or tomorrow. Either way I want Cairo where I know he can't be touched." She said getting up and excusing herself from the table.

That gave me time to talk to Vic. I knew that having Cairo back would soften her a little bit and hopefully she too would forgive me. I wanted shit between us to work and whatever I needed to do to let her see that I was willing to do.

"Vic." I said trying to gain her attention. Instead she took rose from the table and walked out the kitchen.

I was disappointed but definitely wasn't giving up yet. I ended up making a quick turkey sandwich. Just as I was taking the last bite Skye walked into the kitchen and handed me Cairo.

"I text you the details, your flight leaves in an hour and a half Victoria is going to take ya'll to the airport. Ty do not call anyone, I mean nobody. As soon as your flight lands in Miami call me and once you reach the house, call me again." She said kissing Cairo as Vic popped her head in the kitchen and signaled for me to come. I hugged Skye and left out behind Vic.

Victoria

I honestly didn't want to take Ty and Cairo to the airport. Not because I was mad at Ty but because I was in love with him and just didn't want to forgive him for fucking up so easily. Skye knew what she was doing making me take them. He could have easily taken a taxi.

"Vic." Ty called out to me as I stopped at a red light.

I glanced back to the back seat where he and Cairo were and gave him a half smile.

"I'm sorry." He said.

I knew he was. I knew that Ty would never do anything to intentionally put my nephew in harm's way. In fact, he wouldn't put any of us in harm's way; not just Cairo. I was still mad though. I get that he felt some type of way because Ariana lost their baby but shit if my nephew had become collateral damage there would have been hell to pay I knew that I should have let it go because Cairo was safe and back with us. I would, just not at that point in time.

Conversation was at a minimum. For the rest of the ride to JFK the only sounds heard were the tunes that were playing through the radio at a very low volume. I didn't want to wake a sleeping Cairo. When we pulled up to the airport, I got out to kiss my nephew before they headed inside.

"Titi love you Cai." I said after I planted a kiss on his hand. I looked up at Ty, "Have a safe flight." I said and turned to get back in the car. I felt a strong hand grab onto my arm and force me to turn around and that's when our lips met. My brain was screaming for me to back up and continue to play angry but my tongue was dancing to a whole different tune. When we finally did break away from each other I reached up and touched my lip.

Ty smiled and coolly said "I love you Vic." Before turning and heading through the airports door.

I was left there stumped for a minute. He said he loved me. I know he loved me like family all those years but did that declaration of love mean I love you as my woman. I knew it did and that forced a smile on my face and a flutter in my heart. I jumped back into Skye's whip and headed back to her house. With completely happy thoughts. My nephew was safe and Ty had told me he loved me for the first time. Nothing could bring me off that happy cloud. I was going to fully enjoy it even if it was only for the moment. I turned up the volume as Rihanna's song Stay came on and hit the highway.

When I got back to Skye's house I found her sitting in the living room scrolling through her phone like a mad woman. I never saw someone swipe the screen of their iPhone so fast and with so much force ever. I flopped down beside and her and let her know that they were safely at the airport and should be on their way to Miami. She nodded and thanked me without taking her eyes off the screen.

I just left her alone. I sat back and thought about how things would be once all this shit was over. I would have my man and my family, Skye had her man and her son. Things would be good. I just wish it would happen sooner rather than later.

The ringing of Skye's cell phone shook us both. The entire house was silent so the random ringing startled us both. I looked over at her while she took a few breaths before sliding her finger across the screen to answer. I sat up and prepared to listen to the one sided conversation.

"Wassup?" Skye said to the caller on the other line.

There was a moment of silence before she started to speak again.

"No, he don't mess with her anymore why you ask?" I watched her demeanor change as she sat upright and became even more engrossed in the conversation than she was initially.

She popped up from her seat on the couch. "What!" she yelled into the phone.

By this time she was pacing back and forth as she listened to the caller on the other end. Whatever was said had shook Skye to the core. She was irate. When she hung up the phone she snatched her car keys that I sat down on the coffee table.

"Who was that on the phone?" I asked getting up and stepping closer to her.

"It was James. I'll be back sis. Stay put and listen for my call." She said before running out the front door.

Something felt terribly off and I knew calling Skye and begging for answers would get me nowhere. So I sat on the couch and found James number in my phone.

Chapter Five

Ariana

"Fuck baby I'm about to cum!" I squealed as I tightened my grip on his head. My body began to convulse as it released my fluids all over his tongue.

He wasn't fazed, like the pro he was he licked and sucked every ounce of it until he was satisfied that he had cleaned up the mess he had helped create. I was on a cloud; this nigga's sex drive was always on one hundred. He had just finished digging my back out upstairs in the bed room and here he was eating the shit out of my pussy. Who was I to complain?

I looked down at him as he looked at me with a sexy ass smirk on his face.

"I be back shorty I'm going to the bathroom." He said as he got up and headed to the bathroom.

I wanted to move but I was spent. After the multiple orgasms I reached during our sex session to the amazing orgasm I just had from the best head ever I couldn't move if my life depended on it. So I didn't bother. I laid back and caught my breath as I thought about what was next. I needed to get back to my mother's before she started calling me off the hook asking when I was going to pick up Cairo, but I figured a few more hours with my boo wouldn't hurt. Plus I wanted to talk to him about me having Cairo. I didn't want him to find out any other way, because I was really starting to fall for him.

The sound of his footsteps approaching let me know that he was done in the bathroom. I assumed he was cleaning my pussy juice off his face. I chuckled at the thought just as he sat down beside me on the couch and through his arm over my shoulder.

"You good baby?" He looked at me chuckling.

"I am." I said in between planting a kiss on his cheek then on his lips.

He grabbed the controller to his Xbox and started up a game of 2k. I curled under his arm and watched him. I was waiting for the right moment to spring on the information on him. I hoped he wouldn't leave me. I was getting tired of letting niggas in my life only for them to walk right back out. It was time I got what I deserved and get my life back on track. Once I gave Cairo back and got the money my baby and I could move anywhere we wanted and live comfortably. Hopefully start our own family.

Once he was done his game of 2k I knew it was time to talk. Although I dreaded it, it needed to be done.

"Babe." I said in a whisper.

"Yea, shorty wassup?" He said pulling me closer to him.

I took a deep breath and laid it all on the table. Not leaving out one bit of information. If we had any chance of moving forward I had to be honest.

"Fuck you mean you kidnapped their baby?" He barked pushing me away from him.

"You don't understand babe." I started to explain.

"What the fuck is there to understand Ariana? I could give two fucks about Skye or Cam, but the baby ain't have shit to do with nothing. You took shit to a different level." He barked with his vein bulging out his forehead. I didn't anticipate him being that pissed off.

"Calm down. I'm not going to hurt him. Once Ty get up the two million dollars I plan on giving him back." I said with pleading eyes.

The mention of the money calmed him down and his whole demeanor changed.

"Two million dollars?" He asked.

"Yes, do you know what we could do with that?"

Skye

I knew James had no idea what was going on between Ariana and I so I knew he didn't think he was doing much damage by telling me the information he had. What started out as a phone call just to find out if Ty and Ariana were still together led me to that nigga house. I thought back to everything James said I wanted to make sure my next moves were calculated. Everything I did from that moment forward could have dire consequences.

"Yo Skye Ariana and Ty still together?" He asked as soon as I spoke into the phone.

"No, he don't mess with her anymore why you ask?" I was interested in know where the conversation was headed.

"I went to the nigga JR house to pick up some bread and he was bragging about some chick he had just finished smashing. We laughed about it and shit then Ari came skipping into the living room. Look like she shit herself when she saw me, I didn't get into it I just snatched up the money and bounced." He said running down what happened when he went to JR house."

Why JR? I thought as I checked that my nine and made sure the silencer was screwed on before stepping out the Car and heading up the street where his house was located.

I stood outside his front door still was unable to process that Ariana was behind the kidnapping of Cairo. It seems as if from the moment I decided to be with Cameron wholeheartedly my friendship with Ariana was doomed. My heart was heavy because I never in a million years would have thought she would hurt me to this magnitude. I guess she could say the same thing since it was me who made the call to end her life. It was a necessary reaction to things she had done.

I couldn't take it any longer. The more I heard her speak freely about taking my son, the more my finger itched to squeeze the trigger of my nine until the clip emptied. Then there was him, I never thought he had balls. In my eyes he was a soldier who did what he was told and that would always be his position. I never saw him moving up in rank; but there he was in the flesh. Not only showing that he had balls, letting me know they were big. Everyone had an agenda; I kicked myself for it taking me so long to figure it all out. Since I took over I treated him like a brother. To cross Cameron was one thing but me? I treated him like a brother. He made more with me than what Cameron would have ever allowed him to make. It wasn't true what they said about money, I was slowing learning that Pussy was truly the root of all evil.

I grew tired of watching them through the window and listening to them make plans with the money they thought they would gain by requesting ransom. I've heard enough, and at that point I didn't care if I was outnumbered. This was something that needed to be handled and regardless of the outcome I was dead set on handling it. Just as I made up my mind to force my way into the house I saw him making his way toward the front door. I quickly ducked down behind the untrimmed bushes. I pressed my back flat against the house and held my breath until I heard the front door slam and watched as he jogged down the driveway and hopped in his car. I silently cursed because I was hoping to kill two birds with one stone. Surely it would happen another day. I didn't remember hearing the door lock after he stormed off so I used that to my advantage. I stood from behind the bush and slipped on the leather gloves that were tucked into my back pocket and slowly turned the door knob. Just as I expected the door was unlocked.

"*Dumb bitch.*" I thought to myself as I tightened the grip on my nine and tip toed toward the voice I heard having a one sided conversation. I assumed Ariana was on the phone.

I found Ariana sitting in the living room screaming through the phone at someone. She must have been having a bad day except she just wasn't aware how much worse it was about to get. I crept up behind her and pressed the cold steel to her temple snatching her cellphone out her hand in the same motion. After ending the call I contemplated on speaking but I wanted her to see who I was. I wanted Ariana to know I was her personal grim reaper. I wanted to make it clear that she crossed the wrong person.

I walked around the couch bringing myself face to face with the girl I would have given my life for a year ago. The look on her face was priceless, yet and still she gave me a smug look as if she had no worries.

"Kill me and you will never find Cairo." Ariana said staring down at the barrel of my gun.

I let out a hearty laugh. You know one of those grab your stomach, lean over, got stomach cramps because it was so funny type of laughs.

"You really thought that we would never find Cairo. You left him with the most obvious person you stupid bitch." I barked, taking a step closer to her.

I watched the look of defeat overcome her as I placed my gun on the end table. I reached forward and pulled Ariana to her feet by the skimpy puff she called a ponytail. I guess she was that pressed for money she wasn't rocking her normal weave.

I took a step back and through my hands. Although I knew how this would end I wanted to give Ariana a chance to have a one on with me. It's what she always secretly wanted. Her throwing her hands signaled me that she had indeed accepted my challenge. I leaned forward and through a left hook that connected with her jaw causing her to stumble back. She didn't fall but I used the seconds that she tried to compose herself to land blow after blow to her midsection.

I screamed obscenities as I continued to deliver haymakers and hooks, each blow hit the intended target body part. I managed to get Ariana in a headlock, and then I raised my leg and pushed her head down simultaneously crashing my knee into her nose. Hearing her cry out in pain only made me want to go harder. I wanted her silenced for good and I was completely prepared to do it with my bare hands. I had the upper hand until I tripped over the coffee table. I fell backwards onto the floor bringing Ariana down with me.

If I hadn't already knocked the wind out of her she probably would have gotten the best of me since she was now on top. Her blows weren't fazing me she was weak, and she knew it. I trailed her line of sight when her eyes landed on my gun I knew I had to get to it first. Between receiving and reciprocating punches we tussled and knocked over the end table. I crawled towards the gun and Ariana caught my leg. I tried to kick her to break free and continue my pursuit for the gun but it was to no avail. The tussle continued. Ariana delivered a blow to the side of my head that damn near crippled me. In that split second she was able to get her hands on the gun. Giving up wasn't an option so I channeled all the energy I could and lunged towards her. We ended up in an intense struggle me to gain possession of the gun and her to let off the shot that would instantly end my life.

It all started to happen at an extremely fast past. Just as the gun went off I saw a shadowy figure move in the corner of my eye.

"NOOOOOOO!" Victoria screamed.

I hadn't had a clue how she had got there, I wish she would have made it sooner. Thoughts of Cairo flashed through my mind as I felt the blood seeping through my shirt. It only took me a second to realize I wasn't the one who got shot; I hadn't pulled the trigger either. I pushed Ariana's stiff body off of me and found Victoria frozen with the gun still in her hand.

Evidently she was in shock; she had just committed her first murder. I pulled myself up off the floor and walked over to her. Gripping the butt of the gun I slowly tugged it out of her grasp.

"I... I thought she was... I don't know I panicked. I couldn't let anything happen to you sis, which is why I called James. Once he told me what he told you I knew I needed to get to you." She tried to explain.

I looked back at Ariana's dead body and hung my head low. I didn't know what to say to Victoria. One thing for sure though she had saved my life.

"You saved my life Victoria. Thank You." I pulled her into me for an embrace.

"You would have done it for me." She said finally gaining the ability to coherently speak.

"In a heartbeat. We gotta go I'm sure someone heard your gun go off and called the cops." I stated as I walked over to where Ariana's body lay and picked up my gun.

I kneeled down beside her and checked for a pulse, when I was sure there wasn't one I returned to Victoria's side.

"Did you touch anything?" I asked wondering if she had left prints.

"No... I mean the door that's it." She said as contemplation settled in her expression.

I could hear the sirens and knew we were running out of time. We both definitely wouldn't make it out undetected. I knew what needed to be done I just hoped like hell my plan would work.

"Victoria, take these guns. Go through the back. Do not touch anything with your bare hands. Walk a few blocks away and catch a taxi. Call JR and have him meet you at one of the spots. Don't mention anything that happened here. I don't know how you will do it but get his prints on your gun. Wipe yours off first! Here take these gloves."

I quickly removed my gloves and handed them to her.

"Once you got his prints on your gun take the gun and stash it somewhere else don't tell anyone where it is. Please follow my instructions." I pleaded with her.

"I'm not leaving you here to take the fall I did it not you." Victoria said on the brink of crying.

"Victoria do you not hear the sirens? Get the fuck outta here. Now! I will call you!" I walked toward her and shoved her in the direction of the back door.

After a moment of hesitation she left. I pulled out my cell phone and dialed 911 as I headed to the front door. After wiping Victoria's prints off the front door knob with my shirt I sat on the porch and told the police operator my version of what happened. I sat on the porch and went into actress mode. I needed to appear shaken, I needed tears. The only thing that made me sad was the thought of not seeing my son again if my plan didn't work. I thought about Cairo's precious face and how I longed to hold him in my arms and the tears flowed freely.

As four police cars came to a stop in front of the house, I watched as uniformed officers jumped out with their guns drawn. Before doing anything else I put my hands in the air. I wasn't trying to give those cops a reason to open fire. I sat with my hands in the air until I was approached my two female officers who snatched me to my feet and through cuffs on me while the other officers entered the house.

"Why am I in cuffs?" I questioned although I knew I wasn't saying anything until I got to the station.

I heard the officers shout some type of code out which I assumed was signaling them that there was a body.

"You want to tell us what happened that resulted in a dead body?" The tall dark skin police woman stated. She reminded me of Lisa Leslie. She didn't have a cop look on her at all, which made it hard for me to take her serious.

"Not really." I answered nonchalantly.

In order for this plan to work I wasn't speaking to anyone except my mother.

"Have it your way. We'll get the answers we need at the station." The other police woman stated as she grabbed me and walked me toward the police cruiser while her partner read me my rights.

Once they tossed me in the backseat the tall one spoke through the walkie talkie and we were on our way.

Chapter Six

Victoria

"Fuck!" I cursed out loud as I walked down the street to where I had the cab drop me off when I came.

I looked down at my hands and they were trembling. It wasn't because I had killed Ariana; her life meant nothing to me once she decided to fuck with my family. Skye on the other hand had me worried. I couldn't believe I left her there. I prayed that whatever she had planned would work in our favor as I pulled out my phone and searched for JR's name in my contacts. I remembered I needed a taxi so I called first before finding JR's name once again. I hit call and listened as the phone rang four times before he decided to answer.

"What up Vic?" He spoke as if he didn't have a care in the world.

"Hey Jr. What you doing?" I asked hoping he was free and close by.

"Shit. I'm in the east by Tae crib and shit. Just chillin'. What up though you need me?" He sounded like he was a real niggas too bad he was snake.

"Yea can you meet me at the east spot? I'll be there in like twenty." I said hoping that he would come.

"Yea, I got you." He said before we ended the conversation.

I contemplated calling my brother but there was really nothing he could possibly do. In addition to that I knew I needed to stick to Skye's plan. She gave me specific instructions and I knew I had to follow through. I clutched my purse close to me and waited a few more minutes for the cab to pull up. When it did I slid into the back seat and got comfortable. As we headed toward East NY I put on Skye's gloves and buried her gun at the bottom of my bag leaving mine at the top.

When the cab pulled up to the spot I repeated Skye's life depended on it over and over to myself before paying and stepping out the car. I spotted JR's car and knew he was there already. I took a deep breath and headed inside. I definitely forgot to tell him to show up alone but thankfully he did just that. As I got closer to him I had no idea what I was going to say but I knew I needed to come up with something and fast.

"What up punk." I said as I placed my bag on the table he was sitting at.

"Nothing what up? What you doing out here?" He asked eyeing me suspiciously.

"You know my nephew is missing so I'm out here with my ear to the street ready to body any and everything. That's kind of why I called you here." I said reeling him in.

"Shit crazy. Who the fuck would go after Cai? Shit got me fucked up, but whatever I can do to help. I got you." He said. If the circumstances were any different I would have believed him.

"Well I need another burner. The shit I got not going to get the job done." Please take the bait. I thought to myself.

"What you got on you?" He inquired.

"It's in the bag." This was it, make it or break it.

He dug into my bag, biting the bait and pulled out the murder weapon.

"What you damage you thought you was going to do with a nine? Shit can do a little something but you don't know who you up against." He said, inspecting the gun and leaving behind all the prints I needed.

"I know that's why I called you." I said laughing. I'm sure he thought I was laughing at his comment but I was actually laughing at how fucking stupid he was.

"Aight Vic I got you though. Let me make some calls and once I get something I'll hit you up." He said as he put the gun back into my bag.

"Thanks Jr. you a life safer. I'm about to get up out of here though I'm hungry as I don't know what. Don't forget to call me." I said turning to head to the door.

He got up and walked behind me. "Yea I'ma head back to Tae crib whoop that nigga in some 2k but I got you I won't forget." He said climbing into his car.

Cabs ran frequently through this neighborhood so there was no need for me to call one. I stood on the corner and a minute later I was in a cab and heading back to Skye's place to wait for her call. A call I prayed would come with good news.

Skye

The room they had me in was cold as I don't know what. I was tempted to ask for a blanket.

I was a mixture of annoyed and amused by the two cops who were trying to play good cop bad cop. The female detective was trying her hardest to sweet talk me into a confession while her male counterpart was rough, he cursed me out and threatened me with a life sentence. I wouldn't budge; they had no idea who they were dealing with. I was a Law Student, granted I only completed a semester but I knew my shit.

I sat there and stared off into space while they continued to "almost make me crack". That's what they kept saying every time their captain came in to check on their progress. I was growing tired of the antic the back and forth thing was getting old it was time for me to speed the process along.

"I want my lawyer." I said grabbing the pen and pad they had in front of me that was supposed to be used for me to write a confession. Instead I wrote down my mother's name and number and slid it back to the officers.

"Once we call your lawyer we are taking all deals off the table." The male officer uttered.

"Call her." I said and put my head down on the table.

My mother was in Miami so I knew I would be in here for a minute. I was exhausted but there was no way I would be sleeping until I was home. Forty Five minutes later the female detective came back into the interrogation room to escort me to the holding cell.

"I'm owed a phone call aren't I?" I said with sarcasm.

She sucked her teeth and led me to the phone where I was allowed to make one call. Since I knew they were contacting my mother I decided to call Victoria.

"Hello." She answered on the first ring.

"Hey sis. Everything good?" I asked in reference to her handling what she needed to handle with JR.

"Yes, what's going on with you?" She questioned.

I was relieved that she handled what I needed her to do.

"I'm alright. I will probably be in lockup for the night. Depends how fast my mother can get down here. Don't worry about me though I'm good." I stated trying to reassure her that I would be fine. That's when I remembered I wouldn't be able to get any calls. "Did you speak to Ty? Did he and Cairo get to Miami safe?"

"Yes, they touched down right before you called me. He said he got the voicemail on your end so he hit me up. I didn't tell him what's going on though." She explained.

The detective was signaling for me to wrap it up.

"Aight good, I gotta go sis. Go back to Miami now." I said before ending the call.

The detective returned and escorted me to the holding cell that would be home to me for the next few hours.

The cell was colder than the room, and much more uncomfortable I would have rather had been in interrogation getting screamed at by the detectives versus sitting in this small ass cell with three other females, who all looked as if they were prostitutes. My eyes were heavy and I felt myself battling to stay awake, I refused to sleep. The flight from here to Miami was only two hours so I was expecting my mother very soon.

Cameron

I thought I was dreaming hearing Cairo's cries but as the cries got closer I forced my eyes open. Seeing my nigga

Ty walking into the family room with my son in his arms brought over me a feeling I haven't felt in a while. I pulled myself up from lying across the couch and reached my arms out for my prince.

"Where Skye? Where was he?" I demanded. I needed answers and I needed them right then.

"Her and Vic still in New York bro. I really don't have the answers you need. Skye hit me told me to come get him and bring him to you. That's what I did." Ty responded as he walked back out the living room.

I knew he wasn't telling me the entire story but I wasn't going stress it. My little man was home and I was sure Skye would be back soon too so I was content for the moment. I was definitely going to get all the answers I wanted but at the time I just wanted to enjoy having my lil' man back.

"Cai daddy missed you boy." I spoke to him as if he was a big boy.

It didn't matter that he didn't understand. I made it my business to let my son know how much I loved him. That's one thing he would never have to doubt in his life. If I didn't make it to see tomorrow he would know that I loved him.

It wasn't even a whole five minutes before my moms and Skye moms came into the living to see Cairo. They asked the same questions I did but I didn't have any answers for them. That angered them but they suppressed the anger and just accepted the fact that whatever happened, happened, and Cairo was home safe.

Adriana was in the middle of rocking Cairo as he dozed off when her phone started ringing. She handed him to me and accepted the call. Her entire demeanor changed and the look on her face told me that it was about Skye. I felt like I was going to throw up assuming the worse. It's like once one thing got back on track another thing derailed. We just got Cai back now some shit had popped off with Skye. When was it going to end?

My mother and I waited patiently for Adriana to get off the phone and when she did she hit us with some left field shit. Something I never expected to happen.

"Skye has been arrested." She said as she stood up from her seat on the couch.

"For what?" I inquired what could she have done so bad that landed her in jail.

"Murder." She flatly stated before walking off.

My mother went behind her but me I couldn't move quickly even if I wanted to. I was stuck Cairo was sleeping in my arms and I was lost. My girl, my son's mother was facing a murder wrap. Shit really couldn't get any worse. Skye may have had heart but she wasn't built for jail. Definitely wasn't built to face a murder charge. My mother returned to me and Cairo's side in the living room ten minutes after following Adriana out. She let me know Adriana had left and would call us as soon as she had more details. That wasn't satisfying enough I couldn't stomach my girl sitting in a jail cell. I mean it was a much better outcome than what I thought the phone call was about but it wasn't what good in the least bit.

I wondered if Ty knew about this shit, if he did and was keeping it from me it was time for me to dead that nigga. The secret shit needed to be over. It was causing more problems than solving them. My mom's took Cairo from me and headed upstairs. I texted Ty and told him to come meet me in the living room it was time we kicked it like we did back in the day. I never had to worry about Ty keeping shit from me and the fact that I felt like that now didn't sit well with me at all.

My phone vibrated alerting me that I had a new notification. I looked down and say Ty's name on the screen. After punching in my code I went to check the message.

Bro I'm dead ass tired. We'll kick it in the Am.

Type of shit was he on? Now he was avoiding me?

Skye

Nearly four hours later my name was being called. I was sitting straight up on the bench with my eyes glued to the bars. Hoping and praying that my mother would show up. So to hear my name finally being called was like music to my ears.

This was a total different detective from the one who brought me to holding earlier. I guess the shifts had changed. She was much nicer. She didn't grab on me like I was nothing she held onto my arm just to lead the way. I was led back to the interrogation room where my mother was sitting with another detective. The look on her face caused me to drop my head and stare at the Mason Martin Margiela sneakers that adorned my feet. I couldn't bear to see the look of disappointment in her face.

I sat down in the seat beside her and didn't say a word. She cleared her throat and began to give the detectives a tongue ass whooping that only she knew how to serve. My mother really was the best at what she did for a living.

"What are the chargers?" She asked in a very nonchalant manner.

"Murder One. Unless she cooperates." The husky male detective said.

My mother looked at me then back to the detective before cracking a smile.

"Let's go Skye. Officer when you have some chargers that could stick she'll be around." She said before headed to the door. I didn't hesitate to follow her.

I knew that they couldn't hold me there. They had absolutely no proof that I committed a crime. They were banking on me talking myself into a ditch but I knew much better than that. All I had to do was wait it out until my mother came like I did and I was straight. I wanted to head straight to Miami but my mother said it would be best if I stuck around in case I had to go back to the station. I didn't mind sticking around New York a few extra days while they tried their hardest to solve a crime that only Victoria and I had the solution to. Although I wanted to see my baby I knew he was okay so a few more days away were okay with me.

On the cab ride to my parents' house my mother didn't say one word. She shook her leg up and down and I knew exactly what it meant. She was fuming and I understood why. Why wouldn't she be? Her daughter was the suspect in a murder case. Although I knew I would never have to stand up in court the thought still pissed me off so I knew she was pissed off.

When we got in the house my mother wasted no time before ripping me a new one.

"Murder Skye?" She screamed. "This shit has gone too fucking far. My child? Facing a murder charge. What the fuck has gotten into you?"

She drove her fingers into my chest as she continued to scream.

"Mom, I swear to you I didn't kill Ariana. I was there, I know who did it but it wasn't me." I pleaded hoping she would hear me out.

"What the fuck were you even doing there Skye? You do realize how this shit looks?" She questioned lowering her voice. She knew that I wouldn't lie to her so by me telling her that I didn't commit murder calmed her down a bit but she was still upset because I was still facing the charge.

"Mom, I know how it looks but I also know it won't go any further than this." I took a seat on the couch and told her everything that happened. From me ordering to have Ariana killed to how I ended up at JR's house. I even told her that it was indeed Victoria who pulled the trigger. I knew my mother would never throw Victoria to the wolves because she was family. She was my son's aunt and my mother would protect her just as she was going to protect me.

"This is so much to take in Skye. What is your plan? Where is the murder weapon?" She asked.

That was a good question because I had no idea where it was I just prayed Victoria didn't leave it at my house. If I knew the justice system like I thought I did they were definitely going to show up at my place tomorrow with a warrant.

"I don't know. Victoria did what she needed to do and got JR's prints on the gun. I told her once she did that to stash it. I don't know how involved Jr. was with the kidnapping of Cairo but I'm going to leave that to Ty and Cameron to figure out. Like you said mom it has gone too far and I told god if he got me Cairo back I would change and I want to. The gun is just an insurance policy. They won't find proof to send me or Jr. to trial but if it came down to me or him that gun will surface." I explained and hoped that she understood.

"It's been a very long night. Let's get some sleep we'll pick this back up in the morning." She said standing to leave.

"Where is dad?" I called out after her.

"He is overseas doing some scouting he'll be gone for another three or four weeks. We'll keep this from him until he is home we don't want him stressed out while he is away working. Understand?" She stated.

I nodded my head in agreement and she walked off. I wasn't far behind; I headed upstairs for a hot shower then climbed into my bed. Sleep wasn't far behind I was beyond beat.

Cameron

I glanced at the time on the alarm clock and sucked my teeth. It read 6:45am which brought the amount of hours I lied in bed tossing in turning to seven. I hadn't been able to sleep because I was worried about Skye. I knew she was putting up a tough exterior but she was in no way shape or form built for jail. I knew that for sure. I sat up in bed and reached for my cane.

"Dumb ass shit!" I spoke out loud in frustration.

I was over having to get around with my third leg. The cotton like feeling and my mouth made me suppress my frustrations as I needed the cane to go get a bottle of water. After a minute of getting myself together I was up with the assistance of my cane, and headed to the kitchen. I walked in looking to grab a bottle of water and head back to bed but I found Ty sitting at the counter with a big ass bowl of captain crunch.

"What up?" I said opening the refrigerator and getting the water.

"Couldn't sleep." Ty said taking a spoon full of his cereal.

There was commotion coming from the foyer that grabbed both of our attention. Ty got up and started to walk ahead of me as if he needed to assess the situation like I was a little nigga or something. I grabbed my cane and made my way to his side. We walked up on Hector coming in with three other Spanish cats. Two were built like guards so I assumed they were, especially by the way they stood directly behind the old Spanish dude. He had to be Skye's grandfather, I heard about ol' dude before I even knew Skye was he granddaughter I just never met him in person.

"Wassup Hector." I spoke alerting them that we were in their presence.

"Wassup Cameron, this is Skye's grandfather." Hector said confirming my assumption.

"Nice to meet you Andreas." I said reaching my hand out to shake his.

"Did we grow up together?" He asked swatting my hand away.

Nigga lucky he was Skye's grandfather, I was tempted to steal on his old ass. Who the fuck this dude thought he was, Bugsy Siegel? I really couldn't imagine him putting in the work or having the amount of clout he did, he was a pretty looking nigga. He even rocked curly hair like he was related to El and Chico Debarge. He had much more hang time though. Feeling my legs quiver due to me standing for too long I knew it was time for sit down. I said my goodbyes and started toward the living room.

"Actually Cameron I think we should talk." The unknown Debarge brother spoke, stopping me in my tracks.

I pointed toward the living room and hoped he got the message. I wasn't even on no funny shit; I really did just need to sit down. Once I was seated Ty came strolling in behind me, like I knew he would. We didn't know them niggas from Adam, related to Skye or not they were still strangers in my book. Moments after Ty and I were settled in the living room Andreas came in. I thought he would have come along but his two John Cena looking ass guards came with him.

He sat in the chair that was closest to the fireplace and drank from the bottle of water Hector handed him. Andres sat in silence for a minute as he looked over at Ty, then back to me.

"So Cameron, my question for you is how did you let this happen?" Andreas asked, readjusted his position in his seat.

I was confused though. Did he not know all that was going on? How the fuck was I supposed to protect Skye from getting locked up? She didn't even tell me what was going on before she dipped.

"No disrespect sir…" I began to speak but was cut short.

"No disrespect is what a person says right before they disrespect you. Try again, or was your intentions to disrespect me Cameron?" Andreas asked never taking his eyes off me.

If I didn't have love for Skye I would have definitely said fuck that old nigga and went back to my room. It was early as shit and quite frankly I didn't want nor did I need to listen to his shit.

"Nah, it wasn't my intentions to disrespect you. I really don't know how to answer your question though; I'm in no predicament to chase Skye around, state to state. She keeps me in the dark so how much could I possibly do for her." I spoke feeling confident in my answer.

"If you think there was nothing for you to do, you have a lot to learn. Maybe you aren't fit to be in this business. It is your duty, to protect your family Cameron even if you had to do it from your grave. You should always have things in motion to ensure your family is good. Skye should have never known what the inside of a jail cell looked like. You have men there in NYC. Why is that none of them have tabs on her? Is this how ya'll operate? If Skye decides to step down which I will be recommending to her how am I to trust you with my product if I can't trust you with my granddaughter?" Andreas spoke before taking another sip of his water.

I couldn't answer him right away because in a sense he was right. I should at any giving moment been able to call one of my niggas and asked if they had the drop on Skye. I couldn't though. Andreas must have sensed that I didn't have an answer for him because he continued to talk.

At first I thought everything he was saying wasn't beneficial to me or how I ran my shit but he started to really make sense. He schooled me and Ty on shit we would have never thought about previously. Andreas was starting to sound like the Poppy I heard stories about, he was indeed that nigga. I didn't know if it was a good or bad thing having him here in Miami with us. Rumor has it was he only left Panama if it was an emergency and who ever called for that would be sure to suffer dire consequences. Even with having him sitting in my living room I couldn't believe he was actually Skye's grandfather. No wonder it was so easy for her to take over my shit, it was in her blood.

I remember the first time I ever heard about him, it wasn't a pleasant story at all. I had to be about nine or ten years old. My pops was on the phone with Jeff telling him about some Panamanian dude who was supplying the entire east coast and majority of the west. From what I gathered from the conversation was he had some type of VIP client list. Never would he just deal with a regular nigga looking for work. He dealt with bosses, and back then he just didn't think my pops was on that level so he declined his business. My father being the nigga he was took that as motivation to grind harder, he respected how Andreas ran his business. Shit it made sense to me, if you wanted your shit to stay an A1 operation you had to only associate with A1 niggas. It definitely explains why Poppy been around as long as he has. Never served a day in prison and as far as I knew he didn't have niggas gunning for him either. He had beef here and there but he always shut it down resulting in body parts of his enemies being delivered to their family.

That's the story my pops told Jeff, when Jeff wanted to flip out because Andreas denied them. My pops told him about a local dealer named G. G was a young nigga who lived in Canarsie back then. He and his boys actually worked up the courage and tried to go toe to toe with Andreas after being denied also. G took a trip to Panama with his boys ready to put in work. It was the last time him and his boys were heard or seen until their body parts started popping up randomly around the city. Andreas sent a message and the message was heard loud and clear.

Throughout the years I've heard about other encounters that niggas had with Andreas; but didn't get to live to tell their stories. I never thought I would encounter him because my dad had Miguel's family as a connect since back in the day. Our business with the Mexicans was always on point and we never came across any problems until now. I felt like meeting Skye was destiny, not just because I knew she was the one for me but having Andreas on my team is exactly what niggas needed to go to the next level. I just had to show him that I was that guy, definitely had to prove to him the safety of my family came first.

Poppy

Bad enough I had to take an impromptu trip to the states after hearing my granddaughter was arrested. Now I had to deal with these two little shits who knew nothing. I swear, the new school business men handled things way different than how we handled it in my day. However I've heard the stories and I know with a little molding Cameron could really be a force in this business. I planned on guiding him where he needed to be but first I needed to make sure his priorities were intact. I knew he couldn't do much about what happened while he was in a coma but at least now I had him thinking. In the event that something of this magnitude happened again he'll be better prepared.

I don't know what it is that I saw in Cameron, maybe I saw my son in him. Everything about him and Skye's relationship made me think about Andreas Jr. See I made the same mistake Cameron made when I was just starting out in this business. I wasn't ready though nor was I molded for it. My father Renaldo was murdered when I was fifteen years old. I remember the day like it just happened. We had just returned from shopping to find several masked men in our home waiting for us. My mother Amelia was spread out on the couch with her eyes wide open. At first glance I thought she was looking at the scene unfold, until I noticed the tiny bullet hole in the center of her forehead. It wasn't the first time I had seen a dead body but because it was my mother he hurt me deep.

There were words shared between my father and the guys before they gave him the same treatment they gave to my mother. I watched his lifeless body fall at my feet, his eyes were wide open as well and I stared into them while the mask men searched my house in efforts to retrieve money and whatever else they could. Till present day I couldn't understand why they left me alive, I was just thankful they did. It gave me the chance to avenge my parent's death.

I had an uncle who was ready and willing to take over the business upon my father's demise but he was shady and I knew it. I would have rather seen the business fall to pieces than leave it in the hands of a shiest master. I did neither, instead I gathered all the information my father had locked away in various safes and took over myself. No one knew how unprepared I was because I didn't let it show, nor did I speak it. Shit was going well until I met my ex-wife Jennifer, Adriana's mother.

That's when the one and only mistake I've made to date came back to me in the worse way. Like Cameron I thought I had shit under total control. Every one respected me and my men were loyal. I was young, wealthy, and had the most beautiful woman in my bed every night. In my eyes I was untouchable. Jennifer gave birth to AJ a year after we got together, and Adriana one year after that and life was perfect. I couldn't ask for anything more, I had my wife and beautiful children. It was true when they say all good things must come to end, because it did. When Jennifer decided to leave me I got custody of AJ, I thought it was a good idea back then. However, now much older and way wiser I see that it wasn't. For many years everything was okay with AJ living with me until he was sixteen years old and decided he wanted parts. I wasn't going to avoid the inevitable so I allowed it. I felt respected enough, and feared enough that no one would try my son.

During one of my many visits to the states to try to make things better with Jennifer, in hopes that I could see Adriana something went terribly wrong. I returned home to find that my son had been murdered in cold blood. Although I wanted to seek revenge for his death I never had to, someone surprised me and stepped up to the plate. I felt good about that but still carried guilt for what happened to him.

From that day I had a different view on life and how I ran my business. I changed my way of acting and never had the same problem since. If I could I would help Cameron see those things without him having to lose Skye or his son. It was my point for speaking to him in such manner. He may not have understood it at that moment but he would. I would make sure of that.

I schooled Cameron and Ty on a few more things before deciding they had enough. I had only been in Miami for a few hours and didn't want to spend the entire day talking. We had to get down to the bottom of what was going within their organization that led to the kidnapping of Cairo and Skye landing in jail.

"I want to wash the travel off of me and get a few hours of sleep. We'll pick up where we left off a little later on. Oh, and Poppy or Pop Pop will suffice. My school comrades call me Andreas." I said, raising up from the chair I occupied.

We said our goodbyes before Hector showed me to the room I would be staying in for the duration of my trip. Once I was settled in George and Nelson were giving instructions to head back to Panama. They were used to ensure my safe arrival. Now that I was settled in they were no longer needed as long as Hector was around. I planned for this trip to be longer than my normal trip to the states as there was much more that needed to be done. First things first was a shower and a little bit of rest.

Chapter Seven

Skye

As I stepped out of Miami International I sighed a bit of relief. We spent a few extra days in New York while the investigation was underway. They were coming up empty at every corner they turned even after questioning Jr. I knew I would have to face him soon since he was now aware that I was indeed at his house that day but I wasn't worried about that. I was looking forward to it. I really did plan on keeping my end of the deal I made with god. Cairo was home and safe so it was indeed time for me to change my ways. Although the investigation was on going, I pushed all thought about it to the back of my mind. There was no real reason for me to stress over it, I was in the clear. The detectives thought I was guilty but what mattered was what they could prove and that was nothing. I took a few calls from Ariana's mother at first but once she found out that I was a suspect her calling just for a shoulder to cry on turned into empty threats. I didn't have time for that either, thoughts of her were pushed back into the corner of my memory bank with all other details of the incident. I was looking toward my future with my son and hopefully Cameron. It was time for me to get back to being me.

"Mom who picking us up?" I asked as we headed down the street where numerous cars were loading and unloading passengers.

"Hector." She answered not really wanting to acknowledge I was in her presence.

My mother was still very much so pissed over the entire ordeal. I knew that she understood why I did what I did and the position I was in but what mother wanted to defend their child in a murder trial? I respected her being angry so I left her alone. Once we reached Hector I hugged him as he told me it was nice to have me back, before sliding into the backseat of the car.

The entire ride to the house I spent staring out the window thinking about the most important person in my world, Cairo. I couldn't wait to see my baby, hold him, shit I was even looking forward to changing his shitty diapers. The joys of being a mother. That was the moment for me, I thanked god for keeping me alive and sane thus far as well as for bringing my son back. I apologized for all the wrong I've done and asked for his forgiveness. In exchange I vowed to be done. After everything settled I didn't want any more parts of this life. At first I was doing what I needed to do for Cameron and his family; but it was about Cairo now.

When we pulled up to the house I didn't even allow the car to come to a complete stop before opening my door and getting out. I expeditiously approached the front door ready to see my boy. I dug into my Chanel bag to retrieve my keys and let myself in. Walking into the house the aroma of good cooking hit me smack dead in the face.

I migrated to the kitchen to find Mariah cooking and Cameron and Cairo sitting at the counter keeping her company.

"Hey." I said to get their attention.

"Skye, thank god. I'm so happy to have you home. Girl what the hell is wrong with you?" Mariah said while remaining focused on the dish she was preparing.

"I don't really want to talk about it. Cairo!" I switched the subject not wanting to indulge in that story. It happened I was moving forward.

I sat at the counter next to Cameron who has yet to speak to me and reached for my son. He passed him to me before grabbing his cane and rising to make his exit. I really could have cared less at the moment.

"Hi mommy's boy." I cooed at Cairo and planted soft kisses on his cheeks.

His smile was so warm and inviting for a baby, I knew he would have the exact same charm his father possessed.

"Your grandfather is here Skye." Mariah said as if she was giving me a heads up.

I felt my heart sank to the bottom of my stomach. I was prepared to deal with everyone except him.

"What you mean he is here? Like in Miami?" I asked confused.

"Yep he's been here since the day after your mother left to get you. Right now he's out with Ty and Victoria. I don't know where they went." She explained.

Good thing he wasn't home yet I had a bit more time to figure out exactly what I would say to him to keep him from going off on me.

Mariah was on a roll she continued to speak even though I was trying to enjoy my time with my son. She disregarded that. "I don't know what's going on with you and Cameron but ya'll need to fix it."

"They really do." My mother said walking into the kitchen and joining Cairo and I at the counter.

She reached for Cairo and took him out my arms. I didn't protest although I really wanted to.

"We'll talk soon or later." I said not really wanting to have that conversation either.

"You're not busy, go talk now. Fix whatever the issue is because this shit is old and tired." My mother said in a test me if you want to voice.

I knew better to rebuttal, I was already on her bad side and didn't want to bump heads with her again. I kissed my son and headed to Cameron's room where I knew he would be. The door was closed but I didn't care I walked right on in.

Cameron

Hearing someone walking into my room I pressed paused on the controller and looked up from the game of Black Ops I was playing at the moment. My eyes met hers; Skye was still the most gorgeous female walking the earth to me. I just couldn't get past it, she risked her life, even bigger than that the life of our child. For what? I just don't think it was worth it. To make matters worse I'm here and she still think she need to handle my business. Fucked around and landed herself in jail. Type of shit was she on?

"So you really not going to speak to me?" She spoke as she walked further into my room.

I watched her closely, the closer she got the more I felt the urge to snatch her little ass up and fuck all the smart shit I knew she was gonna say right out of her. My dick twitched at the thought of sliding in that, it's been a minute.

"Cameron, really what the fuck is your problem?" She spat.

So much for that.

"Real shit Skye watch your mouth. I know you been running around here the last few months like you was that nigga but that ain't you shorty." I spoke above a whisper but stern enough for her to understand I wasn't in the business of playing games with her.

"What running around like I was that nigga? You got to be shitting me Cameron. Again, I did everything I did for you. Any nigga would have been glad to have a chick like me willing to do any and everything for him. You an unappreciative bastard. You blaming me for what exactly? I'm here, our son was born extremely healthy and he's here. Cairo was kidnapped and I got him back. Me nigga! So what the fuck you up in here mad about. Because you can't run the street like you want? Because you still have therapy? Get the fuck over it Cameron. Niggas get shot every day. You here and instead of acting like you having your fucking period you should be thankful that you get to watch your son grow up. Soon you will be able to chase him up and down a basketball court. Or would you rather never having the ability to walk again. Get your shit together for real. I'm tired of this same routine with you. It's old Cameron. I don't even want a thank you. I don't want you to acknowledge that I did what needed to be done. I just really want you to get it together."

I looked away from her and hit the button on the controller starting the game back up. Before I knew it the controller was snatched out my hand. I looked up at Skye like she was crazy as she through the controller sending it crashing into the wall.

"Don't disrespect me like that Cameron." She barked coming closer to me.

I grabbed my cane and got up off the bed I had to be prepared for whatever she planned on doing next.

"You getting up like you going to do something. Nigga sit the fuck back down." She yelled pointing her finger in my face.

Who was that girl? She definitely wasn't the female I thought I was going to spend the rest of my life with. When did shit even get this bad?

"You think because you spent a night or two in bookings you bad? I don't get how you could be so smart yet so fucking dumb at the same time. Who purposely gets themselves locked up for a crime they claim they didn't commit? That shit was stupid and reckless." I yelled back at her.

"You have no idea what you're talking about that's the funny thing. You swear you know everything. In actually you don't know shit Cameron. In your words I don't get how you could be so smart yet so fucking dumb at the same time. But you know what Cameron…" Her demeanor changed as she spoke. The anger was gone; it was as if she was a different person. I wasn't in the mood for that multiple personality shit so I cut her off.

"Nah I don't know and Skye to keep it trill I don't even care at this point." I said laying my cane back against the night stand and sitting back down on the bed.

She was silent for a minute and we just stared at each other. She wiped away the few tears that escaped her eyes and started to speak again.

"Then we have finally come to an agreement on something because I don't care either. I'm done Cameron. I'm done with this life, I'm done with your fucked up ass attitude, I'm doing allowing you to blame me for shit you should really be praising me for, I'm done with you! Cairo and I are leaving, I'll send him back here to visit you until you are able to come back to New York but I'm not doing this with you anymore. I can't." She walked closer to me bent down and pressed her lips against mine.

The kiss lasted only a minute before she turned away and headed out the room leaving me alone with my thoughts and a fucked up feeling coming over me.

Victoria

"Sis when did you get back!" I dropped my bags and hugged Skye.

Walking into the house from shopping I was totally surprised to see her. I haven't been updated since I left New York. It felt good having her back home. I finally would have someone to talk to about the nightmares I was having. I didn't feel in the least bit bad about killing Ariana but it didn't stop her face from invading my thoughts while I tried to sleep. I shook off the eerie feeling I was starting to feel, focusing on the present.

"Hey sis, I got back a little while ago. Where Ty and Pop Pop?" She questioned looking past me to see if they were coming in.

"They coming, they're gathering all the bags to bring them inside. We went shopping and I went ham for my nephew." I spoke excitedly although I could see she wasn't in the mood. I just was really trying to pick her spirits up.

"You always do Vic. I'm going to grab Cairo and lay down for a bit before I start packing our things." She said as she turned and walked away.

I was totally confused, packing their things for what? I was going to get to the bottom of it and get the answers I wanted but for now I would give Skye the space she needed. I picked up my bags and headed up to my room to put them away.

As I sat on the edge of my bed unpacking the bags from the all-day shopping trip. I had an unsettling feeling in my stomach. I didn't want to talk to Skye because she seemed so upset when we did speak so I decided to go talk to the second source. I walked out my bedroom and descended the steps bypassing Ty and Pop Pop I headed to Cameron's room. The door was slightly cracked so I didn't see the point in knocking I walked in and found him laying back on his bed with his arms across his eyes.

"Bro!" I said as I took a seat on the bottom of his bed.

He moved his arms from his eyes and sat up in the bed.

"What up kid. What you copped me from your little shopping spree?" He asked.

"Nothing." I said with a straight face, even though I was lying.

"Ain't that some shit, just spend up my money and not cop a nigga nothing." He said with a smirk on his face.

I laughed, he knew I was lying. Cam knew me like I knew myself. "You know I did punk shut up. But wassup with Skye bro? She said she was packing her and Cairo's things." I inquired switching the conversation into serious mode.

"Oh she was serious?" He asked in rhetorical manner.

"About what…" I was confused.

"We got into an argument, she said she was leaving and taking Cai but I didn't really think she was for real sis." He said as hurt filled his expression.

"What were ya'll arguing about now?" I needed to know how serious things had become between them. Their relationship was deteriorating at rapid speed it was painful to watch.

I listened to him give me the summary of their argument. As I expected it was my brother's fault. He could be so stubborn at times, but I understood it because I was just like him. I felt kind of guilty that he was blaming her for getting locked up; he had no clue what so ever that she did it to save me. I would bet money that if he knew that he would feel different about the situation. Skye was good to him, matter fact she was good to our family period. She didn't deserve the backlash she was receiving from Cam. Maybe things would be better if she just flat out told him all that has transpired, help him better understand her methods and her reasoning. I still didn't quite understand why she thought it was a good idea to keep most of the things that has happened from Cam.

"Bro, ya'll gotta get it together. If not for ya'll, for Cairo. This family been through too much already. When I say family I include Hector and Pop Pop a lot has happened Cam and they held this family down. I get that your upset that you girl had to bear witness to some of the things that went down but believe me when I tell it everything Skye has done to date was necessary." I tried to explain to him. Knowing my brother it went in one ear and other the other. He would come to terms with everything and accept on his terms and his terms only.

"I really don't care about that I just don't want her to take my son. Who knows when I'ma be cleared to go back to New York I'm supposed to sit around here and not know how my son doing. Or see him when she feel like sending him. Nah I'm not with that. If she wanna go she can go ahead leave Cai though." He stated.

I just nodded my head they both were stubborn as hell but I knew they would get it together. The two of them were meant to be together.

"Well bro, I don't know. I'ma talk to her and see where her head at. Let me go I wanna shower and change before dinner." I said getting up off the bed and leaving the room.

As I turned the corner to go up the stairs I bumped into Ty.

Ty

"Where you rushing off too?" I asked Vic after kissing her on the forehead.

"I'm going to talk to Skye, I need to see what's up with her. She told Cam she's leaving and taking Cairo." Vic said.

I was shocked. I knew Skye was getting fed with how Cam was acting toward her but I didn't think she would get to the point where she would want to leave him. Let alone take Cairo away from him.

"What you think talking to her going to do? You know once Skye sets her mind on something it's a wrap." I said pulling Vic closer to me.

"Stop Ty, and I know that but I think if we all just sit down with Cam and just put everything on the table he wouldn't act the way he does. By us keeping him in the dark about the things that has been going is just making matters worse." Vic tried to get me to see how she viewed things and I had to agree. The secrets were definitely piling on thick when shit finally did hit the fan it wasn't going to be nothing nice.

"I feel you babe. If you can get Skye to agree to sit down with him and put him on then I'm in but I really do doubt she even trying to hear that." I retorted.

"I gotta give it a try, I mean at least at the end of the day if things don't work out I can say I tried. Can you talk to Cam? See if he's up to it." She asked giving me the sexiest sad face I ever seen.

She knew I wouldn't be able to tell her no she was banking on that.

"You know what you're doing Vic. But yeah I got you I'ma talk to my nigga now." I said pulling her in for a kiss. Once we separated I slapped her ass as she headed to go up the steps.

I walked down the corridor towards Cam's room. I honestly didn't know what I would say to my nigga we haven't really sat down and kicked it since last year. So much shit was going on we never had the chance. Vic was right though it was time. I was all for laying shit on the table but there was just one topic I wasn't open to discuss yet. I knocked on his door and waited for him to answer.

"Yo." Cam yelled from the other side of the door.

"What up son it's me, you dressed and shit?" I asked, not wanting to walk in on the nigga if he wasn't proper.

"Yea, come in." Cam responded.

I turned the door knob and walked into the room.

"What up bro." I said taking a seat on the edge of his bed.

We slapped fives and he gave me a head nod. There was an awkward silence between us for a minute until I decided to break the silence.

"So what up man, how's therapy and shit?" I asked trying to get rid of the elephant that was standing smack dead in the center of the room.

"I'm here. So I don't have any complaints fam. Therapy is just therapy not where I wanna be but far from where I started so that's good right." He said looking disinterested in the conversation.

I nodded my head in agreement. When he woke up from his coma he couldn't even feel his legs, at least now he was able to maneuver around even if it was with a cane it beats a wheelchair for life. I decide to kill the small talk and get straight to the point it was either he was going to be down to sit with me and the ladies to discuss everything or he wasn't. Straight like that.

"Aight bro, I'm going to get to the point, you know a lot of shit has went down since you been down some shit you know about but most of it you don't." I began my mini speech.

I could see the look on his face go from complacent to angry as he cut me off. "So ya'll been keeping shit from me. You out of all people son, you supposed to be my nigga. Why ya'll niggas acting like I'ma break into little pieces if ya'll keep it one hundred with me? I'm a grown ass man I can handle this shit." He spoke with anger, which I was expecting. I would have felt the same way if the shoe was on the other foot.

"Cam, it wasn't even like that son. If we told you have of the shit that went down what would that have done? You would have been even more upset at the fact that it wasn't shit you could do about it. You already walking around here acting like you carrying the weight of the world on your shoulder why would we even add to that. We had everything under control bro. If we didn't you would have known." I explained the best way I could and just hopped that he understood.

"Real shit bro, I just wanna relax. Fuck all this talking. Skye wanna leave with Cairo so be it. She better just make sure I see my son often. Niggas wasn't worried about talking to me before now ya'll wanna pow wow. I'm good on that. Ya'll think this shit easy for me?" Cam stated.

I knew he had a lot on his chest so I sat there and listened. Cam was a nigga with pride as most niggas were but he took it to another level, which is why it shocked me to hear him tell me how he really felt about his condition. Cam was never the type to let anyone see him vulnerable but there he was spilling his soul. I felt for him because I could see the eagerness he had in his eyes to get up and handle all the niggas that wronged him but on the same token there was a look of defeat there as well.

"Bro, I hear you. I can't say that I understand what you going through because I don't. What I do know though is that you not alone my nigga. We got you bro. All this feeling sorry for yourself shit is whack son. It's been a few months and look at how much you progressed. You came out speaking like Cairo; now look at you. You going to be aight, I guarantee that. I respect that you just wanna kick back right now and I respect that but soon or later we gotta talk." I stated getting up from the bed.

I walked out the room because I knew Cam and once he said he wasn't doing something he wasn't going to change his mind until he was ready. As I was heading up to Skye's room to talk to her and Vic Adriana handed me Cairo who was knocked out. I looked down at my god son while I walked up the steps and saw Cam. Skye's door was open so I walked in and laid Cairo in the middle of her bed. Vic wasn't in there anymore but I still stuck around and kicked it with Skye for a little bit.

I thought our relationship would have suffered after the shit that went down with Ari but Skye really did forgive me like she said. She didn't hold it against me at all, I knew that was mainly because Cairo was back and he was safe. I just really hopped once Cam found out he would have the same attitude about it. I doubted it but I was ready to roll with the punches. Whatever happened at that point was just going to happen.

Skye and I talked for a minute about her wanting to leave and go back to school. Even though I was on her side about going home and finishing school I couldn't voice that. At the end of the day Cam was still my brother, instead of saying I agreed I just let her vent and get everything she needed to say off her chest. When she was done, I assured her that whatever happened with her and Cam I was only a call away if she or Cai ever needed anything. After all the back and forth today a nigga just wanted to kick back and relax. I left Skye alone with Cairo so I could do just that.

Chapter Eight

Skye

I was glad that Cameron wasn't in the mood to talk about everything because honestly neither was I. I mean I knew soon or later I would have to come clean but after our blow up earlier that day I wasn't ready. My mind was on me getting my life back in order, moving back home with my baby and getting back into school in August. I know things wouldn't go back to normal overnight but the same way I adjusted into this life I planned to adjust back into my old way of doing things. I needed to be better for my son. Speaking of I glanced down next to me to my sleeping baby who was smiling in his sleep. He must have been having a good dream. That made me smile. If it was up to me my son would only know good times. He wouldn't have to endure none of the pain I did these last couple of months. My sole purpose at that point in time was to be the best me I could be for Cairo and make sure he was good. I intended on doing that.

There was a light knock out my door taking my attention away from my prince. I move the pillows closer around him so he wouldn't roll and got off the bed to open the door. It was Pop Pop the only person other than Cameron that I just wasn't prepared to face.

"Hey Pop Pop." I spoke as I reached out and hugged him.

"Hello Nieta!" He said stepping into the room and closing the door behind him.

His warm smile turned into her frown and I knew he too was there to chew me into pieces. Before he could even get to do that I spoke up.

"Pop Pop I know there is a lot we need to discuss but can we talk later or tomorrow. I just want to lie down and rest with my son. I'm extremely fatigued." I said hoping that he would understand and leave me be for a little while.

"I'll see you in the living room in fifteen minutes if that's not enough time to gather your thoughts or whatever you need to do. I don't really know what to tell you." He spoke in a demanding tone before turning and leaving the room.

I should have known he wouldn't get it. I sighed and sat back on the bed. Cairo started to move around and I knew he would be waking up soon. I went to pick him up just as his little eyes fluttered open. Scooping him up in my arms I stared down at my future.

"Mommy loves you Cairo. I promise I will make you proud." I said kissing his hand before he broke out into tears.

"Fat man must be hungry." I spoke softly to him as I headed out the room to make him a bottle.

I walked into the kitchen and my mother already had a bottled ready she knew he would be hungry when he woke up from napping. Even though we weren't seeing eye to eye at the moment I couldn't deny the fact that my mother has been extremely helpful with Cairo. I couldn't thank her enough for that.

"Give me him and go do what you need to do." She exclaimed, while taking Cairo out my arms.

I blew Cairo a kiss before turning and heading into the living room. I walked in to find Cameron, Ty, and Victoria sitting in complete silence.

Victoria

"Wassup sis." I stated when I realized Skye standing in the door way of the living room.

"Hey." She spoke dryly walking towards me and sitting beside me.

No one attempting to speak first. I looked around at the three of them and knew I had to be the one to start the conversation.

"Aight so no one wanted to sit down and put everything on the table so I had to get Pop Pop to get ya'll to come in here and talk. I see none of ya'll want to jump start the conversation so I will." I stated right before taking a deep breath.

It only made sense to start from the beginning so that's what I did. Cam had no idea how hard Skye took him being shot and going into a coma, so I put him on. Every day was a battle for her, not to mention she was pregnant and trying to keep it together for everyone. Of course he felt like she had options but I had to explain to him that there weren't any. The money my mother had in her accounts definitely would not have held us over in the event that Cam didn't wake up so Skye made sure we had money. There was still ongoing beef that Skye set out to squash. I really didn't get the big deal. She was fine, Cairo was fine, the team was together and getting money. Wasn't that the end goal in the first place?

"Aight so you want me to accept the fact that she did all that shit. You want me to look past the fact that she risked her life and the life of my son? Bet, Skye it's all good. I'm over it." Cameron said growing tired of the explanation I was trying to deliver to him.

"You can keep that. I don't care anymore because clearly you still missing the point. I get that you would feel some type of way but damn I really don't deserve the shade. Like you said though, it's all good." Skye said leaning back against the couch as if she had said all she needed to say.

I took that little moment of silence as opportunity to continue to mediate. I didn't feel like I was doing a good job at all but anything was better than us walking around with unspoken tension.

"So ya'll ready to tell me who kidnapped my fucking son and how the gangster over there got him back and ended up arrested or is that shit still top secret?" Cam said before I was able to get my next point across.

I looked at Ty then at Skye, neither one of them budged so once again I was left to give the explanation.

"Cairo was kidnapped by Ariana. Yea she was supposed to be dead but whatever happened with that she wasn't. She took Cairo and once we found out she had him Skye went to get him. You mad at her but she got arrested protecting me. I shot and killed Ariana. Skye came up with a plan in like two point five seconds and got me out of there. If it wasn't for her I would be facing a murder charge right now. So again, you been blaming her and you didn't even know the half Cam." I said letting out a huge breath.

It felt good finally telling the truth about what happened. The looks on Ty and Cam's face were a mixture of disbelieve and shock. There was another moment of silence before Cameron grabbed his cane, stood up, and exploded.

"So you telling me because this nigga didn't have the balls to kill that bitch Ariana, my son was kidnapped and my sister had to commit her first murder." He said taking a step towards Ty who was now out his seat as well.

"Yo Cam for real, chill bro." Ty stated taking a stance, looking like he was ready for whatever.

"Fuck out of here, you telling me the pussy was that good." Cam shouted getting in Ty's face.

I took a step back because if they came to blows I wasn't trying to catch a stray hook. Skye on the other hand wasn't trying to let that scene unfold like that. She jumped up from her seat and stood in between them.

"Cameron stop blaming everyone for shit that happened. It happened, let's move forward. This same dude that you ready to fight is the same dude that murdered his own father to save my life! Yea he messed up by not killing Ariana when he was supposed to; but you really think he would let her live for no apparent reason. Obviously there's a reason everything happened the way it did come on now.

You're too smart to be reacting so fucking stupid. Think! I'm done with this conversation. Get the fuck over it. Ty is family him and Victoria are dating, you wanna scream, curse and hit something right. That's fucking stupid. He has been nothing but loyal to you and he treats your sister the way she should be treated so get the fuck over that too. I'm tired! Because you feel miserable you want to make everyone else feel miserable to. Cut the shit, put on your big man briefs and get the fuck over this shit." Skye shouted before turning and walking out the living room.

There was an intense stare down between Ty and Cam before Cam retreated back to his room.

Cameron

When I got back to my room I fell face first into the bed. I had no idea shit unfolded the way Vic said. They were right; I really was taking my frustrations out on the wrong people. Ty really was my nigga. I can't think of one time where he wasn't there for me or did some shady shit in all the years we had known each other. Skye really had stepped up. Maybe I didn't want to accept it because it's not what I wanted for her. When I met her, the main thing that attracted me to her besides her being fine as fuck was that she had plans for her life. Those plans didn't involve the streets and I needed that. I had my share of street bitches and I wanted different in the girl I would ultimately settle down with.

Her getting involved in my lifestyle was really only her doing what she had to do for me and my family. How could I not respect that? I had to. Vic didn't surprise me much, she been voicing how bad she wanted to parts of the business, but as long as I was able she would have never tasted this life let alone caught a body. Thinking about Vic killing Ari brought me back to Skye. She was ready to take a murder charge to protect my sister. She was indeed the most selfless person I have ever encountered. You don't come across people like that very often so I knew I had to get my shit straight and find a way to get her back. The last thing I wanted to do was to lose half of me and that's exactly what Skye was.

I couldn't be mad at Ty and Vic dating because I had a feeling it would happen. Ty used to make jokes about Vic being the girl he would marry back in the day but I always took him half serious. I knew that when he was serious about a chick he was a good dude so I wasn't worried about him hurting her. If anything it would have been the other way around.

Ty killed Jeff? I really did miss a lot. How did that even present itself? I'm sure he wasn't left with an option but I knew that he wasn't taking the decision he made too well. Jeff wasn't a saint and he definitely had vices but that was his pops at the end of the day. It was really time for me to accept that if I didn't have anyone else in the world I had my sister, Skye, and Ty. They proved that they had me no matter what.

****

After that night Skye kept her word when she said she was leaving with Cairo. I tried to protest but she wasn't having it. There was nothing I could do to get her to change her mind and although I still needed therapy I couldn't be away from my son, or Skye for that matter. It took some convincing but my mother gave and a few days after Skye left we were headed back to New York as well. My mother found me a therapist who would be coming to the house five times a week to help me continue my progress. I was cool with that as long as I was just a car ride away from Cairo and Skye versus a plane ride.

The first few weeks back were cool. I saw my son every day and kicked it with Pop Pop often. He had become much more than just Skye's grandfather. Pop Pop taught me a lot of shit I thought I knew but really had no idea about. It was cool, he was like a mentor or some shit. As far as the team was concerned it was business as usual. Pop Pop kept providing the work and my niggas kept getting it off. To their knowledge I was still away though, I would have loved to see my team but in the event that shit popped off I needed to be one hundred. I used my cane less but still needed it from time to time. So until I was straight it was best if everyone still thought I was still low recuperating.

Chapter Nine

Victoria

I missed Miami but I couldn't lie and say that it didn't feel good to be back home. I missed having Cairo and Skye around every day but it was okay I got to see them almost every day. Cam was in a better space and getting stronger every day. The more he improved the more the old Cam started to resurface. Ty and I were doing great; once Cam got over the initial shock of us being together we told my mother and she accepted it. She loved Ty, so I knew she wouldn't mind us being together as long as he treated me well, and that he did.

The doorbell rang and took my attention away from the movie. I looked and saw that no one else was going to budge so I had to get up and get it. I was mad because Rush Hour was one of my favorite movies. The quicker I got the door the quicker I could get back to the movie. I got up from leaning on Ty and headed toward the front door.

When I opened it I was confused because there was a woman on the other side of the door, one that I had never seen a day in my life.

"Hey can I help you?" I asked her waiting for her to introduce herself or to tell me why she was on my property.

"Hi, I'm Sandra, is Cameron on Mariah here?" She asked in a polite manner.

"One sec." I closed the door and headed back into the family room where everyone was completely wrapped up in the movie.

"Mom and Cam it's a lady named Sandra asking for the two of you." I announced.

"What the hell she doing at my house?" My mother yelled. Her outburst shocked me. She rarely lost her cool like that, which made me even more interested in finding out who this Sandra character was.

"Let her in sis." Cam said much calmer than my mom.

I headed back to the door and opened it to find her still standing there. I motioned for her to come in and I led her into the living room.

"Hello Mariah. Hi everyone." Sandra said as she stepped into the living room.

All eyes were now on her. My mother was eyeing her suspiciously but Cam seemed cool.

"Don't hello me you have nerve coming to my house Sandra." My mother said getting up from her seat.

"Mom relax. How do you know her anyway?" Cam asked just as confused as I was.

"I knew every bitch that your father cheated on me with. I wasn't dumb; Sandra was my friend though until she showed up here pregnant with your fucking brother." My mother blurted out.

Realizing the last bit of information was too much she put her hand over her mouth in a "oops that wasn't supposed to come out" manner. At least now I knew who she was, she was Matthew mother. Why the hell was she at our house? I hope she wasn't coming to ask for money because I'm sure my mother wouldn't think twice about beating the breaks off her up and down the drive way. I knew that by the look she was giving her.

"Mariah, I told you Hassan was not Matthew's father. Yes I did sleep with him but he did not father my child. I don't know what else I could say to get you to believe that. I really didn't come here to hash it out over things we can't change. Jeff knew that he was Matthew's father but refused to tell Hassan. If you want to blame anyone for thinking your husband had a baby on you blame him. He could have put the rumors to rest he had DNA results to prove it. I'm just looking for Matthew. I know that he and Cameron stayed in touch but I haven't heard from him, he hasn't been to atlantes I'm just worried. I didn't have any of your numbers but I knew I could find someone here." Sandra spoke not realizing the bomb that she had dropped had us all ready to pass out.

I looked over to the one who I knew would be affected the most and saw all the color fade from his skin. He had chocolate skin but he turned dry as if all the rich chocolate was drained from his body. I walked over to Ty and put my hand on his shoulder and he pushed it away from him before getting up and walking out the living room.

As I walked out the living room behind him, I heard Cameron telling Sandra that we haven't heard from Matthew either and that he would contact her if we did. I knew that was a lie, Matthew was in someone's dirt napping.

I caught up with Ty leaning against the fountain that rested between our circular driveway. He tried to send me back into the house telling me he needed a minute alone but I couldn't grant him that. I knew he was hurting and as his girl, it was my job to carry that hurt with him. I stood in front of him in silence I knew that when he was ready he would speak to me. I just wanted him to know that I was there for him.

"The only person left in the world that shared my blood. Is dead, and because of me at that. I killed the only two niggas in the world that was my family." He spoke through the tears that flowed freely from his eyes.

I knew that he had been hurting over having to kill his father. He never wanted to talk about it; it was the one topic that was off limits no matter what. I knew that it was only a matter of that before he got tired of walking around with that baggage and let it out. Hearing that Matthew was indeed his brother sent him over the edge. I could even pretend to understand the way he was feeling. How would I have felt if I had to kill my mother and my brother? I mean Ty's dad and Matthew really did deserve their death but Ty didn't deserve to have to live with the guilt of him delivering their death sentences.

"I have nobody Vic! My own mother walked out on me. I probably walked right on by her and not even knew who she was. I don't have grandparents, no other siblings. I killed my pops Vic, I killed my brother. I will never have family."

I had no idea what to say to him, I just wanted to hold him and tell him everything would be okay so that's what I did. I pulled him closer to me and wrapped my arms around him.

"It's going to be okay baby. I'm here for you. No matter what you will have family, you have us Ty and that will never change." I told him while I rubbed his back.

"Nah, that's your fam Vic. Yea, I'm treated like family but it doesn't change the fact that nobody in there shares my blood."

I took a step back from him and stared intensely in his eyes. I was so in love with him that sometimes I couldn't comprehend it. I lift his hand and placed it on my stomach.

"No, you will always have us." I cracked a half smile in hopes that he understood what I was telling him.

He looked like he got it but wasn't really sure.

"You're going to be a dad." Was all I was able to get out before he lifted me off the ground and kissed me.

I knew that in the back of his mind he was still thinking about Jeff and Matthew but at least in the forefront he could focus on the baby that we would be bringing into the world together. He didn't know that I been in touch with a Private Investigator trying to contact his mom. I didn't want to tell him until everything was in stone. I didn't want to get his hopes up just to let him down. So focusing on me and our baby was the right thing to do for the time being. The baby that would forever love him and always be his blood. He was anxious to know when I found out so I explained to him about me having Skye go with me to the Doctor when I was over her house visiting Cairo. He was so happy and I was so happy that I could put a smile on his face during a time when I knew he was hurting.

While we stood there embracing each other I thought back to the day I found out I was pregnant.

I was over Skye's spending some time with her. I had a feeling I was pregnant because my menstrual didn't come twice and it always come. Since I first got it at age thirteen there wasn't a month that it didn't. Even if my cycle changed, it would come early or late but it always came. I was nervous and knew that I could talk to Skye about any and everything so I did just that. She was so happy.

"Let's go to the doctor right now. I hope you are, Cairo needs a playmate." Skye joked as she started putting on her sneakers.

She was serious about going to the doctor the very minute. Even though I told her we would have to wait for ever since we were walking in she still said we were going. So we did. The entire time we waited I bit my nails. I was so nervous, I had become so adjusted to the thought of being a mother I was ready and if I wasn't pregnant I would have been sad.

We were finally called to the back, I thought I was going to have a panic attack due to how nervous and anxious I was. I couldn't focus on anything other than getting the results. Once everything was over we waited.

"Congratulations you are going to be a mommy." My doctor spoke the words I wanted to hear and in that moment

something change. It was no longer about just me, I was going to be a mother. I couldn't wait to meet my prince or princess and I couldn't wait to tell Ty. I knew he would be happy I just wanted the time to be perfect.

"I still can't believe that nigga was my blood babe." Ty spoke into my ear bringing me back to the present and reminded me where we were.

"It's the past baby. I know you carry guilt about your dad and now you will because of Matthew but there is so much more to looked forward to." I verbalized hoping that he would let it go. I couldn't relate because I wasn't in his shoes but I didn't want him walking around moping about something he couldn't change.

He smiled and kissed me again before we headed back into the house. As we were heading in Sandra was leaving. She apologized to us for interrupting and asked once again to have Matthew contact her if we spoke to him. Ty's eyes fell to the floor as he told her he would. Knowing that he couldn't grant her that. Her son was gone forever.

Cameron

I was waiting in the foyer for Skye to pull up. The bomb Sandra dropped really shook shit up and I knew Ty was feeling someway. I made a mental note to talk to him about it later. At that moment was focus was on Cairo. I couldn't wait to see my son, not having him in the same house with me every day was harder than I thought it would be. I got to see him whenever I wanted which was often probably every day even if it was just for a minute but it wasn't the same. When I saw her truck come to a complete stop I walked out the house so I could help her. She stepped out the truck looking fine ass fuck. She didn't even have to try hard. She wore her hair in loose curls that bounced with every movement she made. I smiled at her and she smirked back. I knew she still wanted me but she was just as stubborn as I was. She wasn't going to give in that easy.

"What up baby mother?" I said as I kissed her forehead and headed to open the back door to get Cai out his car seat.

"Hello baby father." She said with a chuckle. I hated her calling me that just as much as she hated me calling her baby mother.

"Cai, look at you boy. You getting big man." I said holding Cairo in my arms.

"Stop being dramatic you just saw him yesterday." Skye laughed grabbing his baby bag.

We walked up to the house side by side like it should always be. When we got inside Skye walked off, I assumed she was going to say her hello's since everybody was home. Cairo and I on the other hand headed straight up to my room where I took off his clothes. He was in the crib for the day so he was straight in just his onesie. I was in the process of taking off my kicks when Skye and Vic came in.

"Dang you just going to hold him hostage?" Victoria said as she bent down and picked Cairo up off the bed.

"Nah, I just wanted to get him comfortable. You can take him to see ma I'll be down there in a minute." I said kicking off my last sneaker.

"Come on big boy." Vic said turning and walking out the room closing the door behind her.

I looked up at Skye as she was unzipping her jacket. She made the simplest gesture look sexy as fuck.

"Why you staring at me?" She said putting her hand on her hip.

"I can't admire my BM beauty?" I let out with a laugh. I knew that would piss her off a little.

"I hate you call me that Cameron." She pouted.

I stood up and walked over to her. I placed each of my hands on her hips and pulled her close. She moved her head back and gave me a look that said she wanted me to let her go but that wasn't going to happen. I leaned forward and kissed her. At first she was hesitant but I felt her body give in to me as she returned my kiss with passion.

I moved my hands from her hips to the bottom of her shirt and slowly raised it and pulled it over her head. I slowly moved my hands up her back and unhooked her bra.

"Please stop Cameron. I don't want to go there with you." Skye's mouth said; but the racing of her heart and the shortness of her breath was singing another song.

I took one of her titties into my mouth and gently pinched the nipple of the other. My dick was extremely hard and threatening to break free from my basketball shorts any minute. Without releasing the hold my mouth had on her titty I reached down and undid her jeans. They were skin tight so it took me a minute to wiggle them over her hips that had seemed to spread after the she gave birth. I had to thank my boy he did his mother's body right. Everything on her enhanced. Her boobs were bigger but not saggy, her ass was fatter, and I bet the pussy was better.

Once her jeans hit her ankles she stepped out of them. All talk of wanting me to stop went out the window the minute her jeans came off. I rubbed her wash board flat stomach which had no visible signs that she had given birth a few months back and trialed my hand down to her box. Moving her thong to the side I slid two fingers into feeling her, feeling her juices flow over my fingers let me know she was ready.

I removed my fingers and sucked them. Before picking her up and tossing her on the bed. I quickly came out of my ball shorts and briefs freeing my piece. I walked over to the bed and slid between her legs stopping when I came face to face with her pussy. I reached up and pulled her down by her thighs and met her opening with my tongue. The initial contact made her squirm; she hasn't been sucked or fucked in a minute so I knew she was anticipating this even if she wouldn't admit it.

I stuck my tongue deeper inside her box and came out quick, repeating that notion over and over had basically trynna shove my head closer to her. I wasn't having it though. I was gonna make her tell me she wanted it.

"Tell me that the pussy is mine." I sang out in the best imitation of Miguel that I could do. She said nothing so entered her with two fingers and flicked my tongue across her clit.

"Aight fuck it." I said sitting up.

"Pleaseeee Cameron, I want to feel you. I need to feel you." She moaned out.

That's all I wanted. She didn't need to ask twice I dove in head first and tongue fucked her brains out. With each lashing I gave her clit with my tongue I felt the walls she had built breakdown. I stuck two fingers back inside her pulsating pussy and fingered her while I gently nibbled her clit. Her body temperature was rising and I felt the heat radiating from her. The grip she head on my head tightened and her legs locked around my neck. Her body trembled as she released a river flow of her juices.

I caught it all as if I was drinking from a faucet. Her body went limp and she sank deeper in the memory foam mattress. I wasn't done with her yet though. Using one hand I flipped her over on her stomach and pulled her up by her thighs. I admired the view of her face down, ass up. With one hand I grabbed a handful of her curls and pulled her toward while I used my other hand to lead piece to her opening.

"Why are you doing this to me Cameron?" Skye yelled out in bliss as she tightened the grip she had on the sheets.

Ignoring he pleas I dug deeper into her cave. I wanted her to feel my shit in her chest and by the way she was trying to get away I know I accomplished just that. Pulling her back toward me and going in deeper she clenched her walls around my dick. That shit drove me absolutely crazy. I thrust in and out faster going deeper each time. Skye was meeting my thrust and throwing her shit right back at me. I felt my shit about to explode so I went harder and I let off my nut deep inside her and didn't pull out until my shit was drained.

I rolled onto my back and without me having to say a word Skye climbed on top of me and slid down on my semi hard dick. Soon as my shit felt the tightness of her pussy it got rock hard again. I looked up at Skye while she bit down on her bottom lip and bounced on my shit merciless. I gripped her by her waist and held her in place while I pumped in and out of her. Each stroke made her moans intensify.

Neither of us was worried about being heard. I pulled down so her titties were against my chest and kissed her as Skye rode my dick.

"I love you Skye." I managed to get out in between kisses.

She reached up and held on to the top of the leather headboard and went up, down, round and round all on my joystick. I felt another nut building up but I wanted her to cum with me. I rolled over still inside her and raised her legs up to her head. Shorty toes were damn near touch her neck.

"Oh my…. Shiiiit Cameron." She yelled out.

I knew she was on the verge of cumin so I went harder and at a faster pace. Her body trembled beneath me just as I let off another load of my men in my pussy. I owned that whether Skye liked the thought of that or not. I stayed in her shit till her convulsions ceased. I leaned over and kissed her, pulled out and rolled over on my back next to her.

"I love you too Cameron." She finally said.

I let that linger while we both caught our second wind.

Chapter Ten

Skye

I got up off the bed and started to put my clothes back on. I wanted to shower badly but I wanted to get away from Cameron just as bad. Not because I didn't love him or didn't want to be with him. Definitely not because the sex wasn't great because it was impeccable; but because Cameron needed to realize that in order for us to move forward with our relationship he had major changes to make. He needed to understand that he could persuade me with great sex. Did it help? Yes. Did it lighten my mood? Absolutely! However, it didn't mend out relationship and until he fully comprehended that our relationship status would remain what it is. We are Cairo's parents, nothing more, nothing less. I was standing there in my jeans and bra when Cameron finally decided to speak.

"You just going to leave?" He asked with hurt behind his eyes.

Through the time of us being together I learned him like I knew myself. I knew when he was hurt. I knew when he was sad, frustrated, tired, hungry shit I even knew when he needed to take a shit. He was my love there was no denying that but I just wanted more. I needed more; Cairo had to see me getting more from him so he would know exactly how to treat his woman when the time came.

"Yes, I told you I didn't want to go there Cameron. We can't get pass our problems by covering them up with the sheets. We really need to work at being a couple again." I said slipping my shirt back over my head.

I felt my hair and knew it was disheveled and all over the place. I didn't my best by patting it down and slipping my arms into my coat.

"I'll call you when I get home." I said before blowing him a kiss and heading out the room.

When I got downstairs, I walked to the living room to say goodbye to everyone and to kiss my son. All eyes were on me I just knew they knew what was going on upstairs between me and Cameron. I played it off though. I gave out hugs before kissing Cairo and heading out to my truck. In the safety of my car I let out a sigh. I missed Cameron so much. More than I was willingly to admit. I wanted to jump out the car and run right back into his arms but I had to put my foot down. A guy would only do to a female what she allowed, and the way Cameron acted toward me when he got out of his coma wasn't going to cut it. He had to come correct if he wanted us to be the family we are supposed to be. Soon or later he would get it right. I wasn't going to stress, at that time things were going fine. I wanted to enjoy it before the next storm hit. I pushed the button my key fob and the car came to life. I couldn't wait to get home to shower and just relax. I missed Cairo whenever he was staying the night with his dad but I couldn't say I didn't enjoy the quiet.

When I pulled up to my building I drove into the residential parking and parked my truck. I climbed out the truck and dug into my bag to retrieve my vibrating phone. I looked down and saw that it was Cameron as I slid to my finger across the screen to answer someone grabbed me grabbed my arm forcing me to turn around.

"What the fuck? Get off me!" I shouted as I realized it was Jr.

"Chill, Chill I just want to talk to you that's it." Jr. said letting my arm go.

"So you had to stake out the parking garage waiting for my return, just to talk to me." I said backing up a little.

I knew I would have to face Jr. soon or later but I didn't think much of it since he wasn't going to jail. There was no murder weapon so the case went cold. Hopefully he just wanted answers and not problems.

"You hard to catch up with. The few times I did see you, you had Cairo I wasn't trying to step to you while you had your kid." He said taking a step toward me.

"I can hear you, you don't need to get close to me to talk. Wassup?" I said growing impatient and wishing I had a gun on me. I would have dropped him where he stood.

"I just want to know what happened that day at my crib. How did you know I Ariana was there? Why you shot her and left me to take the fall for it?" He said looking to his left then back at me.

He was the epitome of suspect at that point I felt like he either wanted to kill me or he was wired and was trying to get me locked up. Neither was going to happen that day. I was sure of that. I knew I had to play my cards right. I was a law student whose career was going to be talking people out of sticky situations I was sure I could get myself out of that. I was also sure that JR had to be dealt with as soon as possible.

"Her mother told me she was at your house Jr. I went there to whoop her ass because she dragged my baby into our drama. But that was it. I didn't get a good look at the person who shot her. We were tussling and she was on top of me. I heard a gun go off and when I felt safe enough to move the person was gone." I lied through my teeth and lied so well that I almost believed it myself.

"I don't believe you Skye. You like my sis you could keep it a hundred with me." He spoke as he started pacing back and forth.

"You right we are like brother and sister which is why I would never leave you to face a murder charge. I was a suspect and so were you my mother advised me to stay low and not communicate with anyone until everything blew over. I'm sorry how everything played out JR; but look at the bright side you aren't locked up are you. Let it go and move on with your life like I'm trying to do." I stated calmly taking another step away from him.

He mumbled a few words under his breath and turned to walk away. I scurried to the elevator and placed the phone to my ear once I realized Cameron had been on the line the entire time.

"Hello." I said into the phone once I was in the safety of the elevator.

"Ty and I are in the car on our way. When you get upstairs make sure your door is locked and stay by your phone I'll be there in a minute." Cameron barked into the phone before ending the call.

As I stepped into my place I closed the door behind me and secured all the locks. I couldn't focus on anything except that if Jr. wanted me dead he had the perfect opportunity. I didn't like the feeling that I was that accessible. It was time for me to move especially now since I had Cairo I didn't feel safe in my own home and I wasn't going to live like a prisoner. I sat on the couch in the living room with my knees pulled into my chest. I took advantage of the silence and gathered my thoughts while I waited for Cameron.

Cameron

Fuck not being ready to hit the streets. The minute a nigga thought it was okay to approach Skye where she rested her head was the exact minute I knew it was time for me to tie up every loose end that was left. I was able to get around without my cane so I was straight. The rest of my healing had to be done on the move. I would continue my physical therapy because I didn't want any setbacks but I was done sitting around the crib. Niggas wanted to see Cam back in action, their wish was my command.

"What made the nigga JR think he could press Skye and not have to deal with ramifications?" Ty said pissing me off all over again.

"These niggas really be forgetting son. Has it been that long?" I asked. It was a rhetorical question though and Ty knew that so he said nothing and continued to drive.

When we finally got to Skye crib Ty found a parking spot and we hurried up stairs to her apartment. I rang the bell and announced that it was me so she would keep calm. As soon as she opened the door I pulled her into me for a hug and stepped inside with Ty right behind me.

"You good?" I asked her although she appeared fine.

"Yes." She uttered, and walked back towards the living room.

I cursed out loud about Jr. being brave pressing her at her spot as I followed behind her. I didn't know where she got all the strength she possessed but she was really one of the strongest people I knew. She barely let niggas see her sweat but I knew she was pissed.

"I really think he was wearing a wire or something." Skye said as I sat down beside her.

"It don't matter, that nigga should have left well enough alone. When I get through with him he going to wish he did." I shouted.

"What's the plan bro?" Ty asked coming from the kitchen with a bottle of water in his hand.

"Ya'll don't have to do anything. I got this one." Skye said causing me to look at her crazy.

She sensed that I was confused by her statement and went on to explain herself. Skye never told us about her and Vic getting JR's prints on the gun Vic used to kill Ariana until that moment. She said they figured the less people who knew about the gun the better the chances it would work if the time presented itself. Skye didn't even have a clue where the gun was located. She wanted it that way. Being alert and seeing how she handled certain situation really made it easier for me to come to terms with the things that happened while I was in the coma.

Skye really did know what she was doing. She was the smartest of us all because all her moves were calculated to the T. Rarely did she act on impulse and that's what kept her alive and out of jail. Niggas in the game could definitely learn a lot from her. I couldn't even front shorty had me cheesing hard as hell as she broke down how she planned on using the gun against Jr. At first she didn't want to do it any there really wasn't a need for her to. She and Jr. were both off the hook. No gun no case; he had to fuck it all up by pressing it now he was going to pay the ultimate price.

"Damn sis that was a smooth ass plan. How your ass get so hip to this shit?" Ty asked, acknowledging that it was indeed a good plan.

Skye smiled and leaned her head on my shoulder. I rubbed her cheek and told her I loved her. Together or not I didn't really see myself not loving her. We been through so much in such a short period of time and instead of packing up and running for the hills she stuck it out with a nigga. How could I not love her? Not to mention she gave me Cairo.

"I'll handle it from here Skye. I'll get the location of the gun from Vic and get it to that nigga Detective Harris.

You won't have to worry about Jr. In the meantime I think you should move back into the long island crib, and I think you need to look into getting a gun license. It's a process but I rather you have a legal piece on you at all times than some illegal shit and you get caught up on a gun charge." I explained.

Skye wasn't feeling the idea of moving back into my house but she compromised and said she would go stay at her grandfather crib in Staten Island. Of course I would rather have her laid up at my crib with me but her getting out this spot that niggas knew of was better than nothing.

"I'm going to take a shower. Can you stay the night with me?" Skye asked as she got up from the couch.

"Yea, I'll stay. Cairo with mom anyway. Let me kick it with Ty for a minute." I replied.

Skye said bye to Ty before heading to the room for a shower.

"How you want to handle this son?" Ty asked, once Skye was out of earshot.

"When you get back to the house find out from Vic where the gun at. After that we will pay that nigga Jr. a visit. I'ma body him but leave the gun behind let the pigs bury him and the case at the same damn time." I said leaning back against the couch.

Ty agreed that it was a solid plan and said he would hit me up once he got the location on the murder weapon before heading out. After locking him out, I went and joined Skye in the shower.

Chapter Eleven

Man

If felt good to be back. A nigga missed the life; sitting back with a shit bag attached to me wasn't how I wanted to spend the rest of my life. It was music to my ears when my doctor announced that I was getting the shit removed. Only thing I could think about was hitting the streets and getting back to the money. While I was down my niggas stayed low, they couldn't afford any run in's with Cam boys until I was up and ready to pop off. Unfortunately that gave them fuck boys the chance to slide in and take over my blocks. I wasn't too concerned about that though because I was back and ready to go hard.

I was a little fucked up when I found out Ari got bodied. I knew it was coming though she was reckless and always on some other shit, shorty was bound to slip up. I was more so tight that I didn't have a source anymore. It was other ways to get information but the way shorty ran her mouth made shit much easier for me. I had a few tricks up my sleeve and couldn't wait to put them into effect.

I stepped out the cab as it came to a complete stop in front my house. Nobody knew I would be home today. I wanted my return to be a surprise to everyone. As I walked towards my crib I heard someone calling my name.

"Yo Man." The voice called out.

I turned around and spotted my nigga O jogging up the block. When he reached me I dapped him up. O was my brother like my mother's kids, like the nigga Hov said. I had mad love for him because he always had my back. It didn't matter what it was he was always ready, and proved himself to be loyal on many occasions.

"What up bro." I said leaning against the gate that surrounded my building.

"Shit nigga, why you ain't let us know you was coming back to the hood today?" O questioned while he pulled out a black and mild.

"Just wanted to pop up ya know. So what's been up kid?" I questioned already knowing the answer.

As expected he told me all the shit I already knew. It was time for Cam and Ty to take that one way trip to the cross roads. All this back and forth shit was getting whack. I just wanted to stack my bread, fuck bitches, and live comfortably. I couldn't do that peacefully with them niggas still breathing the same air as me.

"I hear you boy. I'm back though and I'm ready to lay them niggas down for good and get back to this paper. Feel me?" I stated as me slapped fives signaling we were on the same page.

"Well nigga, you already know whatever the plan is count a nigga in. I gotta a lil' shorty to feed." He said taking a pull of the black.

"Word speaking of which how your daughter doing?" I asked.

"Getting big and bad ass fuck man." O replied.

We shared a laughed and walking around the gate to the entrance of my building.

As we were walking into the building my cousin and her home girl were coming out. I hadn't seen her in a minute so I shocked.

"What up big head!" I shouted pulling her in for a hug.

"Hey cuz, auntie didn't tell me you were coming home today. It's good to see you up and doing well." My cousin said giving me and O a once over.

"She didn't know, but yea it's good to see you too. What you doing out here?" I asked.

"Visiting for a bit. You know I had to stop by to check your mom. I gotta go thought Man call me nigga the number is still the same." She said before hugging me and making her exit.

As she walked away a light bulb went off forcing a smile on my face. Shit was about to be over real soon.

Chapter Twelve

Ty

The sun peeked through the curtains and did a dance routine on my face forcing me to open my eyes. Vic's leg was draped across me and her head was on my chest. I looked down at her and smiled thinking about the crazy ass sex session we had the night before. The thought of it made my dick hard. I contemplated starting my day by taking a dip in her box but I knew I had other shit that needed to be handled. I kissed her forehead before sliding out the bed.

"Where are you going?" She asked with her eyes still closed.

So much for not waking her up.

"My bad baby I didn't want to wake you up. I'm about to shower and shit I gotta head out handle some shit with Cam." I said walking toward the bathroom until I remembered I needed something else from her. "Yo Vic, where you stashed that gun?"

My question caught her of guard because the look on her face was a mixture of being busted and confused. She let the question marinate before finally answering me. I was shocked at the response she gave. When did she and Skye learn all these tactics and shit they were using? Shorty hid the gun in the nigga back yard. Yea, it was reckless going back to the crime scene but at the same time it was smart as hell. If the location did get out it would still fall on Jr. I nodded at her and smiled before going in the bathroom to shower and shit.

When I got out the shower Vic was curled up in a fetal position sleep. I really must have worn her out the previous night. Shit I was still tired myself but getting at the nigga JR was important. I quickly got dressed in a Vinnie's Styles crew neck, a pair of Trues and slipped on my wheat construction timberlands. I kissed Vic before heading to Cam room to get him changing clothes and dipping.

The entire drive to Skye crib I hopped that Cam was really up to putting in work. It's been a minute and he still have his physical therapy sessions and shit I just wasn't convinced that he was ready. It was too late though; there was no turning back or changing his mind. In the event that he wasn't ready all I could do was hold my nigga down like I had been doing.

As I pulled up to Skye building a charger was pulling out, freeing up a parking spot. I pulled in as soon as there was enough space. I hated having to park blocks away and walking down so the spot was clutch. After parking I killed the engine and headed upstairs.

Skye

I erotically through my head back and clenched my eyes shut. I leaned back on the counter putting all my weight on my hands and grinded forward to meet Cameron's thrust. What started out as making something to eat turned into a hot and steamy sex intermission. I didn't have any complaints though.

"Oh, my…." I moaned out as Cameron hit my spot repeatedly.

There was knock out my front door. I was totally oblivious to it and blocked it out. I was too close to going over the edge.

"Damn babe!" Cameron grunted, as he thrust in and out harder and faster.

I tightened the grip my legs had on his waist as I felt my climax building. The knocking was persistent. They either had to wait or go away.

"Fuckkk Cameron!" I screamed as my body convulsed and released all over his manhood.

The pulsating of my walls sent Cameron over the edge too. He pulled me close and released his men inside me. We took a few minutes to catch our breath before Cameron leaned forward and kissed me before playfully biting my lip.

I totally forgot about the visitor at the door until I heard the knock again.

"Who the fuck is that?" Cameron asked looking at me sideways.

"Babe I don't know." I said jumping off the counter.

I pulled my robe close around me and tied it before heading into the foyer to get the door.

"Who?" I asked as I approached the door.

"Finally sis, open the door."

I immediately recognized the voice, it belonged to Ty. I open the door and he playfully mushed me.

"Ya'll niggas really can't stay off each other." Ty said in between laughs.

He knew what he walked in on, I didn't need to respond. I let out a low chuckle before closing and locking the door once he was inside.

"Make yourself at home bro. Your boy will be out after his shower." I stated.

"Aight, here I brought the nigga some clothes. I know he don't have no up to date shit here." Ty exclaimed handing me the bag that houses Cameron's change of clothes.

I took the bag from Ty and headed to my bedroom. I heard the shower running, so I opened my robe let it fall to the floor and joined Cameron in the shower.

"Cameron I love you." I declared.

Cameron turned to face me and pulled me close to him.

"Skye, I really am sorry for everything. You have been nothing but the glue that my family, no that I needed to keep everything together and I appreciate that. We are not where I want us to be in terms of our relationship and I take the blame for that completely. We will get there though I promise you and when we do it will be better than it was. I love you and Cairo more than anything in the world baby girl. If you don't know anything else, know that Skye." Cameron retorted before leaning down and kissing me.

No more words needed to be shared. We took turns washing each other off and exited the shower. Once we were in the bedroom I gave him the bag of clothes Ty bought over and we both got dressed.

"Babe I gotta run out with Ty and handle some shit. Cairo at home with ma and Vic. I really don't want you staying here so you should head to Staten Island or go to my house." Cameron said as he stood in the door way ready to go.

"Cameron don't worry about me. You be careful if you start feeling weak or anything please go home. Don't be reckless you have our son to think about." I said in a serious tone.

Cameron nodded at me letting me know that he acknowledged what I said to him before walking toward be planting a kiss in my forehead and leaving out. I was worried, actually that was an understatement for how I felt. I knew Cameron and Ty were out for blood and I just wished they used the gun to get him locked up. That's all that was needed. Feeling the need to vent I grabbed my phone and immediately called Victoria.

"Hey Sis." Victoria said answering the phone on the first ring.

"What you doing?" I inquired.

"I just finished getting dressed. What's wrong? You sound stressed. What my brother do now?" Victoria asked as if she just knew it was Cameron related.

I informed her that he didn't do anything to me per say before giving her a run down on how I was feeling. I knew that no matter what Victoria would side with me. She too was worried about the men and wished they just took the easy way out. That wasn't in their DNA though. JR was bound to get dealt with in a barrage of gun fire. It's just the way Ty and Cameron handled things.

"Sis, don't worry about it. That damn murder looming over us going to die today with Jr." Victoria stated with venom dripping from her tone.

She answered the phone so cheerful, and switched up her demeanor that quick. She and Cameron were definitely related. I really hoped that she was sitting this one out. I badly wanted parts but it was important to me that I kept my promise to god.

"Sis let them handle it." I stated hoping she would let whatever thoughts came to her mind go.

"I love you sis, I will let them handle it because I know they got this. I also know that when they catch him it's a wrap so breathe easy. I gotta go though." Victoria said before ending the phone call. I let out a huge sigh before falling back on my bed. It just was a never ending cycle, it was always something! The shit was never going to end. I was completely convinced.

Victoria

After hanging up the phone with Skye I grabbed my car keys and headed outside to my whip. I wanted to kick it with her more, shit I wanted nothing more than to be by her side while Cam and Ty handled JR but I had something else on my plate. I was running late for my meeting and couldn't get sidetracked. For the past few weeks I had been working with a Private Investigator. I was hoping to find any bit of information on Ty's mother. I watched him hurt over not having her or his father and it killed me. I promised myself that I would do all that I could to reunite them. I didn't plan on stopping until there were absolutely no options left.

I pulled up to Amy Ruth's in Harlem where I was schedule to meet with my PI. Luckily for me there was a parking spot right out front. I through the car in park before jumping out and heading inside. I browsed through the patrons in search of the familiar face. I spotted him sitting in the back of the restaurant and headed in his direction. When he felt my presence he looked up and smiled.

"Hello Victoria." Mr. Reynolds spoke as I took a seat directly across from him.

"Hello Mr. Reynolds. Please tell me you have some good news for me?" I asked jumping to the point.

"In fact I do." I said sliding the manila envelope across the table.

I wasted no time emptying its contents and thumbing through all the paper work. My eyes landed on a photo of a woman who was the spitting image of Ty. She and him shared the same smooth Chocolate skin, a deep dimple on each side of their cheeks, the exact same almond shaped brown eyes. That woman was indeed his mother. Her name was Erica Robinson, and she lived out in Long Island. The paper work documented her as being a nurse at North Shore Hospital. She was in our reach all this time. I shook my head as I flipped through the rest of the pages.

"The information your mother provided was extremely helpful in terms of helping track her down. What isn't mentioned in the documents is the fact that she isn't married and lives alone with her daughter who is around thirteen or fourteen years old." Mr. Reynolds said as I stared down at the papers.

"What should I do now?" I asked him unsure of what my next move should be.

"You must decide if opening this box is worth it. You may recover things that will change that young man's life for better or worse. You have to be prepared for either before you decide to move forward." Mr. Reynolds stated.

He was absolutely right; I knew that finding Ty's mom would shake his world up. I just hoped it would be for the better. I knew one thing though I wasn't going to rush into contacting her. I needed to think the entire thing through before I made a move. When and if the time came I knew where to find her. I dug into my wallet and handed Mr. Reynolds the envelope with the remainder of the money he was owed. I thanked him for his services, places all the documents back into the manila envelope and left. I needed someone's sound opinion on what to do next so I headed to Skye's place.

Chapter Thirteen
Cameron

"Bro, I need your solid opinion on some shit before we do this." I said to Ty as we sat in the car four houses down from JR's.

"Wassup?" Ty said looking over at me.

"What you think we should do? I know you ready to ride and just body this nigga because that's what I want to do but what is your gut telling you? Should we just let the nigga Harris find the gun and leave it at that or what?" I asked him, expecting his honest unbiased opinion.

"Wassup with you? You never second guess yourself Cam." Ty stated. I could tell he was concerned.

"Yea but I wanna get shit right with Skye and I know that's how she wanted to handle it. She and Vic went through the lengths they went through to make sure shit wouldn't fall back on them. I just feel like we should trust them." I stated looking at the wallpaper on my phone which was a picture of Skye and Cairo.

Ty didn't say anything back. Instead he grabbed his nine out the glove compartment and placed his hand on the door handle. That was all I needed. As long as I had my nigga and he had me shit would go in our favor. We hopped out the car with our weapons concealed and walked in the opposite direction of his house. We weren't trying to risk being seen by any one going in the front so we planned to use the back door.

"Bro, remember Skye said she think he was wearing a wire. Don't say my name while we are in there, and we gotta put that nigga down before he recognizes one of us and says our name." I told Ty as we crept across his backyard grass.

"I got you." Ty retorted

As we stood outside of his backdoor we slipped on the ski mask that was in our back pockets. I reached for the door knob and of course it was unlocked. The nigga hadn't learned his lesson about leaving his door unlocked? He was going to learn that day. Back to back Ty and I entered the house and searched each room on the lower level there was no Jr. We scaled the wall at we tiptoed up the steps.

We followed the sound of running water that led us outside the bathroom. I looked back at Ty and nodded before kicking the door in. As soon as I had the line on JR I let off two shots. One pierced his chest dropping him instantly and the other was a stray. I walked closer to the shower and pulled the curtain back. I looked down at him as he squirmed and clutched his chest. I watched the water mix with his blood as it flowed down the drain before raising my gun and emptying the clip in his face.

I admired my handy work for a second before Ty and I back peddled out his crib the same way we entered. When we got back to the car I told Ty my plan about putting Harris onto the gun that killed Ariana in a few days. The NYPD needed to think I had no idea JR was dead. It was a legit plan and I was able to sigh knowing that JR and the threat of someone finding out who was really responsible for what happened to Ariana was nothing but a memory.

I turned on Jay Z's Magna Carta Holy Grail album and we headed back to Long island.

Chapter Fourteen

Cameron

The shit with JR and the murder weapon worked seamlessly. I hit up Harris a few days after JR's body was discovered and told him one of my niggas put me on and said JR killed Ariana, and told him where he stashed the gun. Harris told me JR was dead, which wasn't news to me and that he would get on finding the gun. It only took a few hours before he called me back and let me know ballistics were a match to the gun and it was now a closed case.

It was a chill day. Cairo was in Staten Island with his mother, and Vic was visiting them. Ty and I decided to hit the mall. I wanted to cop Skye some shit. She told us she didn't want any gifts or a party but that wasn't cool with me. Skye deserved the world and as long as I was alive and breathing I would provide just that. We still weren't together but I wasn't trying to pressure her. I knew that when she was ready and in the space she wanted to be in moving forward she would definitely come back.

"Well look who it is!" I heard a female voice as Ty and I browsed the women section of Bloomingdales.

I turned around toward the direction of the voice and that's when I saw her. It's been a minute but she hadn't changed a bit. She got thicker, but she wore it well. The extra weight complimented her 5'6 inch frame well. She had smooth dark skin, beady brown eyes, shoulder length hair that she always wore with long bangs that almost covered her eyes. She reminded me of a thick Kelly Rowland. She couldn't hold a candle to Skye but he was still pretty.

"Wassup Aaliyah?" I finally spoke as she approached Ty and me.

"Hey Stranger, wassup Ty?" Aaliyah said playfully slapping him in the arm and then hugging me.

"It's been forever shorty how you been?" I asked moving her back with my hands on each side of her.

"Yea I know, and I'm good. Out here visiting the family for a little bit. I missed you Cam." Aaliyah said flashing me a gorgeous smile.

I didn't know how to respond to her. The decent thing to do would have been to tell her I missed her too but I didn't. I haven't had the chance to miss her. Since I met Skye she has been the only female who I thought of constantly outside of my moms and Vic.

I didn't wanna hurt Aaliyah's feelings though because we had history together. She was like my first serious girlfriend back in High school. We met freshman year on like the third day of school she was transferred into my math class. At the time I was messing with a ton of bitches but it was something different about Aaliyah. She was quiet, and classy. A real step up from the hood chicks that seemed to flock to me.

After spitting a couple lines to her after class we exchanged numbers. We hit it off instantly and kicked it for the next four years. I still messed with other chicks, I was young and wasn't really trynna settle down. Aaliyah was cool with it, she knew she was my main chick and came before the rest. Things with us probably would have progressed but our relationship ended abruptly when her mom's decided to up and move to Ohio.

If it was now we probably could have made it work, but we were teens who knew nothing about making a long distance relationship work. My mind was on getting as much pussy as possible and I couldn't do that if she was in Ohio; so yea there was no chance. Seeing her now didn't even make old feelings surface. It just went to show how in love I was with Skye. Thinking about her made me smile.

"What you smiling at boy. I guess it's safe to say you missed me too." Aaliyah said snapping me out of my thoughts.

I laughed with her. Making her think I was busted when in actuality I just wanted to see Skye.

"It was nice seeing you though A, we gotta chill before you head back to Ohio." I said getting my phone out my pocket so we could exchange numbers.

I handed her the phone, she handed me hers. After punching in our respective numbers we switched back. She hugged us, made a promise to call and walked off with the girl who was accompanying her.

Man

I was scrolling through my phone book looking for a bitch I could call over and smash, when I landed on my cousin's name. I smirked and thought might as well start putting my plan in motion. After hitting her name I put the phone to my ear and listened to it ring. I was ready to hang up when she finally answered.

"Wassup Man." She said into the receiver as she answered.

"What up Cuz, what you doing?" I inquired. Even though I wanted to skip the small talk and get to my point. I didn't want her to think I was using her though.

"At the mall with Mika. Guess who I ran into?" She said sounding all in love and shit.

"Who?" I asked not really caring.

"Cameron and Ty, I haven't seen them in so long. They still look the same. Cam still fine as ever. Not that you care about his looks or nothing." Aaliyah replied chuckling.

Was I that lucky? No wonder she was excited. She and Cam dated back in high school and I was sure she was still feeling him. Since Aaliyah opened the door mentioning Cam I took that as my cue to put her on to my plans. At first she seemed a bit hesitant but once I explained that they were the ones who killed my brother, uncle max, and shot me she was all for it. Just like I expected. The good thing about using Aaliyah to help was that she was my blood, unlike that bitch Ariana her loyalty would always be to me.

After discussing the plan in details we ended up kicking it a little long before deciding to link up later in the week once she had made progress. Once I ended the call with her I hit up my niggas letting them know we needed to meet up. Before anything else I had to put them on game. I needed them to be ready when shit went down which had to be very soon seeing ass niggas on my end was staring. We had to get back to the paper and fast. A little more patience and everything would fall into place. I was ready!

Chapter Fifteen

Skye

It's been months since the last incident and it honestly felt good to have a semi normal life again. I was looking forward to being back the next semester and everything going well. Everything with JR was behind us so I was thankful for that. We knew Man was somewhere in the cut waiting to strike so we were always on alert. I had finally got my gun license and had a legal piece that never left my side. I felt safe know that I could protect myself and my son need be. Speaking of Cairo, he was growing so fast right before my eyes and found new ways to amaze me every day. I was just getting accustomed to the way things were but I had an unsettling feeling that trouble was lurking and would soon show its face. I couldn't give too much energy to those thoughts. I focused my energy on doing well and school and being the best mother I could possibly be.

I walked around the Staten Island house that I stayed at with Pop Pop and Hector, doing a little cleaning with Kirk Franklins "I smile" playing in the background. It was a Sunday morning ritual that I had picked up since I had been trying to get my life back on track. I wasn't the most religious person, and didn't attend church nearly as much as I should have but I know and believe in god. Playing gospel on Sunday mornings settled my spirit and made me feel his presence. It worked for me.

"Todays a new day, and there is no sunshine." I sang out as I walked over to get my vibrating phone off the coffee table.

I looked down and saw that it was Cameron calling. I smiled as I answered. We weren't together but we were in a good place. There was a process and we were taking the necessary steps to rebuild our foundation, we wanted our next shot to be the last so we had to do it right.

"Heyyyyyy Sir." I sang out into the phone.

"Wassup love? What you doing?" He asked before answering his own question. "Oh never mind I hear the music." He said laughing.

I flopped down on the couch and kicked it with him for a little while. I really was happy with the direction we were moving in. We were talking about everything under the sun, laughing, and flirting. Cairo was with him for the weekend so he had an earful to tell me about what Cai was up to that weekend. It was always something new with Cairo; he possessed the character of one way beyond his months. It was such a joy watching him grow and hearing about the time he spent with his dad made my heart smile.

Cameron was far from perfect but he was an amazing dad and I could not have picked a better suited person to be my son's father if I was able to hand pick one myself. He didn't let the bumps and our road affect his relationship with his son and I really did appreciate that.

"So I'll see you tonight right?" Cameron asked although I already promised to have dinner over his house.

"As promised. I'll be there." I stated reassuring him.

"Aight, I love you." He pronounced.

"I love you too." I declared, ending the call.

The remainder of that day went smooth; I had a chance to do all the things I couldn't do when Cairo was home. He demanded every ounce of my attention, I didn't mind one bit. I loved everything that came along with being his mother. Once my housework was completed, and laundry was put away I retired to the shower.

After a long day of cleaning and doing laundry the steamy hot water that rained down on my body was much needed. Even after washing I lingered in the shower just enjoying the feeling until I remembered I had to go to Long Island for dinner. I didn't want to keep them waiting because I wouldn't hear the last of it. I stepped out the shower and grabbed my towel off the towel rack before wrapping it around my body.

After entering my bed room I dried off and applied Carol's daughter lotion to my body. I sauntered over to my dresser to retrieve a lace bra and thong set and slipped into them both. In nothing but a bra and thong I walked over to my closet to look for something to wear. It was just dinner with the family so I didn't need to get too dressed up. I settled for a pair of jeans and loose fitted shirt from Zara. After putting on my clothes I stepped into a pair of Tory Burch flats. Cute and simple is what I was going for and I was confident that I succeeded.

I grabbed the Tory Burch bag that matched the flats I was rocking and transferred everything from the bag I wore the previous day into that one before headed out.

I was busy singing along to Justin Timberlake's Mirror when my phone started ringing. I looked down and scrunched my face because I didn't recognize the number. I didn't hesitate to answer it though.

"Hello." I answered as I turned down the music.

"Skye, Skye, Skye, how are you?" Hearing the male voice that was all too familiar sent chills down my spine.

"Miguel." I said dryly contemplating hanging up.

"Don't sound too excited to hear from me. I told you I'd be in touch. I'm glad you got your son back and that everything is well with Cameron." Miguel said letting out a low chuckle.

It bothered me so much that Miguel seemed to always have one up. He knew all of moves probably before they were even made.

"What is that you want from me?" I asked hoping he would get to the point.

"Pick up where I left off with Cameron." He said matter-of-factly.

"That's not going to happen Miguel." I stated.

"I think you're a smart girl, so you know that answer will not suffice." Miguel retorted raising his voice.

"Well that's the fucking answer you will be getting. Don't call me anymore with your bullshit. You asked for the money you got the money now please leave me the hell alone." I shouted before ending the call.

I wasn't going to let Miguel ruin the mood I found myself in. I was going to have dinner with my extended family and all thoughts of him needed to be pushed to back of my mind. I grabbed my things and headed out the door.

Ty

Vic and I had just left out of the bathroom from having a quickie. I hoped that the fam didn't hear us. Well, even if they did it, was whatever. Vic was showing now so they knew we were fucking. Unfortunately, as the pregnancy progressed her symptoms worsened. If she wasn't eating, she was sleeping. I had to slide in the pussy whenever opportunity presented itself. It just so happened that it was right before family dinner.

I was walking through the foyer when Skye came waltzing through the front door. It was good seeing little sis getting back to her old self. She was happy with the woman she was reverting back to and happy with the direction of her and my nigga relationship was going so I was happy for her.

"What up Sis!" I said.

"Hey bro. Where my boy?" She asked after hugging me. I knew she was referring to Cairo but I wanted to fuck with her a bit.

"Big boy or little boy?" I said trying to hold back my laugh.

"You a clown Ty." Skye said slapping my arm.

"Nah but he in the dining room, you all late and shit. Got us starving." I said as we both walked in the direction of the dining room.

It felt good having the family all in one setting again on some peaceful shit. Even Hector and Pop Pop were there for dinner. They both had become an important factor of all of our lives and shit felt complete when they were there. Adriana and Mariah were just wrapping up dinner while we all sat around making jokes and enjoy each other's company.

Once the food was served it seemed as if all talking had ceased and we dug in. Dinner was the shit as usually and had everyone on the verge of falling asleep once we were done. The ladies retired to the living room while Cam and I cleaned up the dining room and the kitchen. Pop Pop and Hector was supposed to help us but they dipped out for business right after dinner.

By the time we got back to the living room Skye was ready to head back to Staten Island with Cairo. Although Cam pleaded with her to stay the night she didn't budge. We all knew once she made up her mind about something that was it. That night was no different. Vic claimed she wanted to spend time with Skye she went home with her. Cam and I just kicked it for the rest of the night playing video games and shit.

Chapter Sixteen

Skye

I was happy Victoria decided to go home with me. It was nice having her to hang out with. Living in Staten Island I've had more lonely nights than I had become accustomed to. I had Cairo but there wasn't much he and I could do. Not like we could hold a conversation about how our day was. Nonetheless I loved every minute of being a mom. Pop Pop and Hector were always on the go so they were no use in terms of keeping me company either.

We strolled through Americana mall, Cairo was laid back in his stroller enjoying being chauffeured around and Victoria was right beside me.

"We about to swipe the strip off the back of my brothers card sis." Victoria said making a credit card swipe gesture with her hands.

I laughed at her, partially because only she would say something like that and partially because it was true. Even though Cameron and I weren't together he made sure Cairo and I was good in every aspect. He knew that I had plenty of cash and never needed a dime from him; but that didn't stop him from being a provider. Anything I purchased with Cameron's money was always for our son. Cairo is his responsibility not me, so I didn't deem it necessary to spend his cash on myself.

Our first stop was the food court. Being pregnant Victoria felt the urge to eat everything her eyes landed on I couldn't complain because I was the same way when I was pregnant with Cairo.

"What you trying to eat sis?" I asked her as we browsed the variety of food options.

"I'm straight with a pretzel for right now." She responded pointing over where Auntie Anne's Pretzels was located.

I was happy with her choice; it wasn't an official mall trip unless getting an Auntie Anne's pretzel was involved. We headed over to the booth and waited on the line till it was our turn. I ordered a two plain pretzels for Victoria and I but I made sure hers was unsalted definitely wasn't trying to have her pressure shoot through the roof during her pregnancy. I knew Cairo would want to eat my pretzel so I ordered him unsalted pretzel bites. Something he could munch on while we shopped.

After paying for our pretzels we were on our way outside to the strip where the stores were located. Americana wasn't like the normal mall where you went inside a building to find a bunch of different stores. The stores there were located outside similar to the setup of an outlet. As soon as we stepped out into the August heat I spotted the Ralph Lauren store. That had to be our first stop. My son wore so much Ralph Lauren you would think he was a baby model for them. I considered it.

Once inside the Ralph Lauren store I picked up everything I laid my eyes on that Cairo didn't have yet. There was just so much cute things for little boys and my son deserved to have it all. As long as Cameron and I were able that's how it would always be for Cairo. We even picked up a ton of things for Victoria's baby. They were neutral things like onesies since we didn't know the sex yet. By the time I relieved Ralph Lauren of most of their baby stock I had a tab of over fifteen hundred dollars.

"Cairo is too damn spoiled." Victoria said as we made our way to the next store.

I heard her but I sort of tuned her out as I zoomed my focus on the Spanish guy that I spotted near Auntie Anne's. I could have been a coincidence that he too like Ralph Lauren but to be safe I tapped the dug into my Chanel bag to make sure my Nina was tucked away in case she was needed.

"It's ya'll fault too. Everybody I spoils this little boy. Your baby next." I retorted still eyeing the Spanish man suspiciously.

Victoria and I laughed as we went in and out of a few of our favorite stores. We stopped my Tiffany and Co where I purchased my mother and Mariah earrings just so they can know that I appreciated them. We were walking out the Juicy Couture store when I spotted the Spanish man again. There wasn't that many coincidences in the world, I didn't want to make Victoria panic so I made up an excuse.

"Girl, let's head home, we could hit the rest of these stores when we don't have Cairo. I don't want my baby to catch sun burn." I laughed nervously. Hoping she didn't catch wind that I was indeed panicking my damn self.

If it was just Victoria and I, I would have been fine. Having my son with us made shit a lot more risky.

"I saw him sis. I didn't want you to panic." Victoria revealed to me.

I should have known she wasn't oblivious that we were being followed. I didn't respond to her I just smiled and focused on making it back to my truck. Once we were at the car I wasted no time strapping Cairo into his car seat and double checking that he was secure. I didn't know what was going to happen but I knew that I would die protecting my son. Acting as if everything was normal Victoria and I climbed in the driver and passenger seats of the truck and was ready to roll.

As I maneuvered through the parking lot I instructed Victoria to get my gun out my purse in case we needed to use it. I would have rather her to have been ready versus fidgeting to get the gun in the heat of the moment. Just as I stopped at the red light which separated the parking lot from the ongoing traffic a black Tahoe slammed into my side of the truck. I yelped out in pain and slammed my foot on the gas sending my tucking flying into traffic.

"What the fuck!" Victoria screamed out just as the bullets began to beat into my truck.

My entire left side was on fire from the impact of being hit but I had to get to my son. I sped through traffic ass our assailants trailed us letting loose their weapons. I swerved on the highway barely missing the Camry that had the right a way. I glanced back at Cairo who was releasing a piercing scream.

"Mommy is here Cairo." I said trying to soothe him with the tone of my voice.

My hands were trembling as I tried to maintain control of the wheel. The gun fire didn't cease. I turned my head just a bullet went flying through my window missing my head by inches.

"Victoria, I don't know how we going to do this but I need you to get control of the wheel. I gotta get Cairo." I screamed over the sound of guns blazing.

If it wasn't for my impeccable driving skills we all would have looked like Swiss cheese. I screamed at Victoria to snap out her trance and to get her to listen to my instructions. I waited for her to grip the wheel before attempting to climb into the back seat.

I heard the back window shatter and a burning sensation in my back. I knew I had been shot as the pain intensified. I couldn't stop though; I fumbled with the buckles on Cairo's car seat and was hit again. I cried out in pain but and knew I would fight to my last breath to protect my son. Freeing Cairo from his car seat I picked him up and laid him on the floor between the front seats and back seats. By that time I was hunched over him going in and out of consciousness.

I heard Victoria calling out my name and I thought I was responding. I felt my lips move but there was no sound. The pain I was in was overpowering every last one of my senses. Cairo cried and squirmed beneath me so I knew he was okay. I was in the middle of praying when the truck jerked and everything went black.

Victoria

I struggled to open my eyes; they were heavy and felt super glued shut. I fought to remember what happened until the beeping sound coming from the machines alerted me that I was in the hospital. Flashes of the incident came back to me at once causing me to panic. Was I shot, where was Skye and Cairo? Was my baby okay? I fought a little harder before my eye lids finally let me take over and fluttered open.

I attempted to move my head left then right but the excruciating pain in my head stopped me. I felt around the side of me for the button that I knew would be present. There was always a button for patients to hit when they needed a nurse or their doctor. Once my fingers ran across it I used what strength I had and pressed the button. Moments later a short chubby lady who looked to be of Indian decent came walking into my room.

"Look who is awake." She said flashing me a warm smile.

I attempted to speak and she stopped my grabbing the pitcher off the table beside my bed she poured some water into the cup and came closer to me.

"Take slow and steady sips." She instructed as she held the cup to my lips.

"I'm nurse Singh. Do you know where you are?" She asked sitting the cup back down on the table.

I nodded yes. She proceeded to ask me did I remember how I landed in the hospital and I nodded yes again.

"Good I'm going to step out and return with your doctor." She turned to walk away and I grabbed her arm. It wasn't rough but it had enough force to stop her in her tracks and she turned back around towards me.

"My baby?" I asked with tears welling up.

She pointed to one of the screens which had wires that were pasted on my stomach.

"This machine monitors the heart rate of the baby. At first we were worried because the baby was indeed in distress but once we stabilized your pressure the baby's heart rate stabilized as well. He or she is doing fine. I assure you. Please let me get your doctor so he can fill you in on everything else." She smiled and sauntered out the room.

I prayed that Cairo and Skye were okay as I lay back with my eyes closed.

"Hello." The male voice brought me out of my thoughts.

"Hi." I said weakly as I struggled to sit up.

He approached my side and helped me.

"I'm Dr. Jan. Can we start with you telling me your name?" He asked.

I nodded before opening my mouth to speak. "Victoria Carter."

"Okay Ms. Carter you suffered a mild concussion during the accident. Apparently you banged your head on the dash board. There was no damage done to your brain but you will have a headache for a little bit. Your baby is doing fine; we will keep you for a few days just to make sure nothing changes. There are officers outside who want to speak to you but they won't come in unless I give them the okay. Only way I will do that is if you tell me it's okay." He explained.

"I was with my sister, and my nephew please tell me they are okay." I spoke disregarding his comment about the cops. I had no intentions on speaking to them.

"I didn't treat the young lady you were brought in with however I can get you an update on her condition. The child is fine; he is in the children's ward with someone from child protective services. He…"

Hearing him say that Cairo was with CPS pissed me off. So much so that I cut him off right in the middle of his explanation.

"Please we have family. Please call them don't take my nephew." I pleaded.

"They have no intentions on taking him Ms. Carter it is protocol because he was unattended while you and your sister were being treated. Nurse Singh please get the information for her relatives and give them a call please. Ms. Carter I will be back with the information on your sister. I will also have them bring your nephew up here so that you can see with you own eyes that he is well."

I was relieved; Cairo was okay I just had to be patient for news on Skye. The Nurse handed me a piece of paper and a pen. I quickly jotted down me and Skye's first and last name as well as the numbers to Cameron and my mother. As she went out the room to make the call I felt the pain medicine taking affect again and dozed off.

Chapter Seventeen

Cameron

I looked over at Aaliyah and she was snoozing. I laughed because I told her that whack ass movie was going to have one of us knocked out. I grabbed one of the pillows that I was leaning on and slid it underneath her head. She moved a little but didn't wake up. I stood from the seat I was occupying on the couch and walked into the kitchen where I found Ty stuffing his face.

"Nigga you sure Vic pregnant and not you?" We shared a laughed.

He couldn't debate with what I said because he knew he ate a lot. If it wasn't for our work out sessions and impromptu ball games my nigga would be on his Rick Ross shit.

"You and Liyah was looking pretty cozy my nigga." Ty spoke between the sips he took from his water.

"Nah it's not even like that. She cool, but she already know what it is with me and Skye. She don't even try to overstep." I said opening the fridge and grabbing a bottle of water.

"For now." Ty said nonchalantly.

I sat down across from him and opened my water. I knew Ty wasn't feeling Aaliyah but what he said made me think. The conversation about me and Skye came up a lot during the time I been kicking it with Aaliyah. I made it very clear each time that I had all intentions on being with Skye. If Aaliyah didn't take me serious she would only end up being hurt in the end. I was never one to string chicks along so I kept it one hundred out the gate. We were cool and I wanted to keep it on a friendship level. The minute I felt like she was trying to overstep that, she was getting cut the fuck off.

The vibration of my cell phone brought me out of my thoughts. I dug down into the pockets of my cargos and got it. I glanced at the number and thought about ignoring it because it wasn't a contact already saved in my phone. I went against that and slid my finger across the screen before pressing it to my ear.

"What up." I spoke into the phone.

"Hello, is this Cameron Carter?" The female voice spoke.

"Yea, who is this?" I asked.

"Hello Mr. Carter. I am a Nurse Singh from North Shore University Hospital. We have two patients here by the names of Victoria Carter and Skye Lewis. Your name was giving as a contact. Are you of any relation to them?" She stated.

All I heard was Vic and Skye's names everything else was blocked out.

"Are they okay? I'm on my way." I declared signaling for Ty to follow me.

"I can't give any details of their conditions over the phone but will gladly assist you once you get here." She declared.

I thanked her before walking in the living room and waking up Aaliyah. I apologized for interrupting her sleep and explained it was an emergency. We all left out the house together and hopped in my truck. I thought about, I couldn't show up to the hospital with Aaliyah. Skye knew I was kicking it with her but still I would never disrespect her in that manner. Aaliyah was never around when Skye or Cairo was present.

"Liyah, my sister and my shorty in the hospital. I mean Skye." I started to explain.

"I hope everything is Okay Cam, I'll call a cab. It's not a problem. Just text me and let me know they both are well when you can. Later Ty." She answered before climbing out the back seat.

I appreciated that she wasn't one of those chicks who just loved drama. She understood her position in my life. Don't get me wrong I never treated her like she was nothing because we did have history; but I didn't treat her like she came before Skye. That would never happen.

Once she was away from the car I started it up and Ty and I were on the way to North Shore. I explained to him what the nurse told me while he texted my mom's and Adriana. Pop Pop and Hector were in town so I had him text them as well and tell them to meet us at the hospital.

I barely parked when I jumped out the car and ran into the emergency room. I didn't know what to think especially because Cairo was with them and his name was never mentioned. I spoke briefly to the receptionist before Ty and I were escorted by security to the trauma unit. I spoke briefly to the nurse at the nurse's station who happened to be Nurse Singh the one who made the call. She was nice but I didn't have time for the pleasantries.

"There was a child with them." I uttered to her as she led Ty and I to Vic's room.

By that time we were there at Vic's room and I heard Cairo as I stepped into the room. He was sitting on some woman's lap and Vic was looking directly at him with tears in her eyes. I automatically picked up Cairo not caring that the woman protested.

"This is my son." I shouted as I walked over to Vic's bed and stood beside Ty.

"Skye needs you Cam." She said before gesturing for me to give Cairo to Ty.

I did just that and back peddled out the room in search of the nurse who had showed me to Vic's room. When I found her I asked if she could take me to Skye and she kindly obliged. I walked into Skye's room and felt as if my world was spinning out of control. There were two doctors standing beside her bed and as I got closer I saw that she was lying on her stomach and her leg was in a cast.

"Are you a relative?" One of the doctors asked briefly taking his attention off of Skye.

"I...I I'm Cameron. Her..." I stuttered to get my sentence out. I was relieved when he began speaking over me.

"She has been asking for you." He said stepping back from Skye giving me space to be by her side.

I put my hand in hers and she squeezed it.

"How is she?" I asked looking at the doctors for answers.

He took a deep breath before giving me a breakdown of Skye's condition. She was shot twice in her back; one bullet was through and through while they had to perform surgery to remove the other. She had a broken leg and a fractured rib. *What the fuck happened?* I thought to myself while trying to mask the emotional breakdown I was on the verge of having. I thought I heard all there was to hear when the doctor that was closest to me put his hand on my shoulder.

"The baby is fine right now but we are not sure that it will go full term. Ms. Lewis went through a lot of trauma and the baby may be affected." He uttered in a sincere manner.

I felt the hold she had on my hand tighten and I knew that she was hurting ten times worse than I was. I had no idea that she was pregnant but I knew for a fact it was my baby. We weren't together but I hit it on a regular basis, and I knew Skye wasn't fucking with anyone else. That shit hurt me to the core. Just the thought of our baby not making it was a hard pill to swallow. If the baby could just hang in there, I made a silent promise to him or her that I would do everything possible to make the rest of Skye's pregnancy stress free. I couldn't wait to get the full story and bury whoever the fuck was behind this shit. The doctors excused themselves and left me alone with Skye which I was thankful for. We needed the time alone. Even if we spent it in silence we needed it.

I tried to let go of her hand and she tightened the hold she had on mine.

"I'm not leaving you shorty. I just wanna grab the chair so I can sit next to you. I promise I'm not going to leave you Skye." I reassured her.

She slowly let go of the grasp she had on my hand and I walked a few feet away and grabbed a chair. Placing it directly beside her bed I took a seat and put my hand in hers once more. I stared at her and watched the tears streaming down her cheeks. I couldn't suppress mine any longer so I cried with her.

"I'm sorry." Was all I could say?

"Cai…" She tried to speak.

I leaned closer to so that I could hear her clearly. Her voice was low and raspy but I knew she was asking about Cairo.

"He's okay baby. He's perfectly fine, Ty has him. Want me to get him?" I spoke.

She nodded her head yes and let go my hand signaling that it was okay for me to leave for the moment. I quickly maneuvered through the hospital until I got to Victoria's room. I saw she was smiling so I knew she was okay, plus Ty was there so I didn't need to linger around. I grabbed Cairo and headed back to Skye's room. When we walked in she was knocked out. I was kind of glad because I knew as long as she was up she was in pain. At least she could relax for a bit even if her sleep was short lived.

Skye

I woke up in severe pain. I tried to move but my attempts were futile. I took a few breaths to get the pain under control and fluttered my eyes open. The first thing I laid eyes on made me smile. Cameron was sitting right beside my bed with Cairo in his arms. Cairo was knocked out, Cameron had his eyes closed but I knew he wasn't sleep. There were voices coming from behind me but I couldn't bear the pain of turning my head to see who was there. I knew once voice was my mother's she spoke above everyone else.

"Cameron." I whispered, gently squeezing his hands.

His eyes shot opened and he leaned forward with the vein bulging out his forehead. "She's up." He announced. "Are you okay?" He said returning his attention to me.

I nodded my head and closed my eyes for a second. *"Thank you god."* I said to myself before opening my eyes again. I had to thank him because I was looking at his gift to me, and he was safe and unharmed. I would get shot all over if it meant protecting my son.

"Skye I need to know about the gun they found at the scene. Please tell me it's the one we got registered." My mother asked as she walked from behind me and stood next to Cameron.

I thought about the gun and sighed in relief because it was indeed the gun Cameron insisted that I had registered, and it was clean. I gave her a half smile and nodded my head yes.

"Thank god baby girl, I just couldn't deal with this on top of a gun charge." She said bending over kissing me on the cheek. As she stood up straight she continued to talk. "I know you are not up for it but we need to know what happened Skye."

She was right; I didn't want to talk about it so I ignored her motioned for Cameron to come closer.

"Yes, baby what you need?" He questioned.

"Can you please get the nurse? I want to turn over and hold Cairo." I exclaimed.

He nodded before standing up and handing Cairo to my mother. His seat was taken by my dad. If I could move I would have jumped right into his arms. I was so happy to see him. Lately he has been burying himself in work to the point where he had to be gone weeks at a time. I didn't understand and wanted answers but in that moment I was just happy to see his face.

"Hi Princess." He said moving a lose strand of hair out my face.

"Daddy I'm so happy to see you." I whispered.

"Rest Skye, I'm not going anywhere." He stated.

"Harvey, she needs to tell us what happened." My mother Voiced.

"Not right now Adriana." My father asserted.

He shot her a look of contempt and I saw defeat in her eyes. I had never seen that type of interaction between the two of them and I wanted to know what the problem was. Maybe dad found out the secrets mom been keeping. That would have surely rubbed him the wrong way. I don't know though, I just didn't see my mother indulging in that information with him and I knew for sure Pop Pop wouldn't.

"Dad, what's going on?" I inquired.

He looked up at my mother and frowned. "You care to share with our daughter why I'm pissed off Adriana or should I." He said turning his head back to me.

My mother went to talk but was cut off by the voice I recognized to be Hector's.

"Not here Harvey." Hector said stepping closer to my mother.

"If I wanted your opinion I would have asked you for it. Why the fuck you hear anyway?" My father spoke as he stood from his seat.

Hector went to respond but was interrupted by the nurse asking them to clear the room so she could clean my bandages and help me turn over.

It took her a little over twenty minutes to clean me up and help me turn over on my back. Leaning back on the wounds that were surgical stitched closed hurt like hell. I had to deal with it because I wanted to hold my son in my arms. Having him so close and not being able to touch him was hurting.

When my family returned Cairo was wide awake so I was happy. I was saddened to see that my father was no longer there and neither was Pop Pop. I asked about their disappearance and my mom told me that Pop Pop went to talk to my father outside and that they both would be back. That made me feel a bit better. Cameron placed Cairo in my arms and I winced in pain. My rib was on fire but I was dead set on pushing through the pain to hold my son.

"Mommy is so happy that you are okay Cai." I whispered to Cairo before kissing him on his forehead.

Cameron had returned to his seat and laid his head on the edge of my bed. I reached down and massaged his head. I knew he was stressing over the condition I was in on top of the news that our baby may or may not make it full term.. I couldn't help but think if I would have never turned down Miguel's proposition this would have never happened.

Pop Pop

I knew why Harvey was frustrated, I understood completely. However, he needed to get a hold of his emotions and deal with the situation at a later time. Skye was in no position to deal with her parent's drama and neither was I. Everyone made the decisions they made and now we all had to deal with them. Harvey included.

"Nieta, are you ready to tell us what happened?" I asked walking back into Skye's room and moving closer to the bed.

"Not really Pop Pop, but I know that I have to." Skye said handing Cairo back to Cameron and sitting back.

As she sat back on the bed she winced in pain. I was ready to murder whoever put her in this situation. I took a lot of things lightly but messing with my family, money, or livelihood was not one of those things.

"The sooner we know the details, the quicker we can handle it." I said gently rubbing her hand.

I stared intensely at Skye and noticed that she was in contemplation, or maybe she was trying to prepare what she would say in her head. I wasn't going to rush her but I was growing impatient. While I was outside speaking to Harvey, I made a phone call back home. Reinforcements would be arriving soon and by that time I wanted to have enough information for them to get the job done and head back to panama.

"Well, a few weeks ago I got a call from Miguel." Skye started to explain.

"Why wouldn't you tell me Skye?" Cameron said with a look of contempt written across his once neutral expression.

"I didn't want you getting worked up, or back into beef with him over something I could have handled Cameron... At least I thought I handled it. He told me he wanted me to get your organization back in business with him. I didn't even need to think about it my answer was no off the back. He made a few threats and I hung up on him. That was the end of that. Today Vic, Cairo, and I were at Manhasset shopping and I spotted a Spanish dude following us. I knew it had to be Miguel's people because we not beefing with any other Spanish team. I just wanted to get Cairo to safety that's all. I knew Vic and I could handle ourselves. It happened so fast, like a scene from bad boys II. We were in the car headed out the parking lot and a truck slammed into mine. Although my side was on fire I knew I couldn't stop. That's when the gun fire started. We had to think fast I let Victoria get control of the wheel while I climbed in the back to shield Cairo. That's when I got shot..." Skye paused, swallowing the lump that formed in her throat.

She struggled to keep her tears at bay but inevitably lost the battle. "If I didn't climb back there, Cairo would have been shot." She cried.

I pulled her close to me gently and rubbed the back of her head while she cried in my chest.

"It's okay Nieta. Cairo is fine, you saved him. You protected him, like a mother should." I said in attempts to console her.

I looked over at Cameron who hadn't said a word and saw that he was on the verge of exploding. I knew it was because of two things; one his girl and son was put in harm's way, and two it was his beef which caused it.

"Miguel?" Adriana questioned after picking her brain trying to figure out where she knew the name from.

It was what I feared. Unbeknownst to any of them Adriana and Miguel had history.

"Not now Adriana." I uttered shooting her a glare that told her to keep her mouth shut.

"That mother fucker is dead!" Adriana shouted disregarding what I told her.

Skye looked at the scene unfold and was completely confused. Her mother's outburst would surely open Pandora's Box. Skye would have questions no one was prepared to answer.

"I should have killed that motherfucker too! I just knew I should have!" Adriana screamed as she paced the floor.

I shook my head knowing it was time to put all cards on the table. The secrets we held in the dark could no longer be kept as they were forcing their own way out into the light.

Skye

Watching my mother's reaction to finding out this was Miguel's doing really confused me. How in the world did she know Miguel? Even if the name was familiar, how did she automatically know it was the Miguel she knew? What did she mean by kill him too? I wanted answers but something nagging at me told me I wouldn't like nor would I be able to handle the answers. Thinking about it made me look around the room again. My father never returned, and that saddened me.

"What's going on here?" I asked looking at Pop Pop for answers.

He sighed and looked as if he was ready to speak but the words didn't come out. I looked from Pop Pop, to my mother, then over to Hector. Even he looked as if someone killed his puppy. The tension in the room was so thick it could have been cut with a knife.

"Mom." I called out weakly.

The medicine was starting to take effect again but I fought it as I began to get drowsy. I wasn't going to sleep until I got answers.

"What exactly do you want to know Skye?" My mother said sounding as if she really didn't want to indulge in the conversation.

"Everything." I stated.

She came closer to my bed and grabbed my hand. I mentally prepared myself for what she was going to say. I knew it had to be serious just by the way they were all acting. She had my undivided attention; Cameron's as well.

There was no way I could have expected or been prepared for what my mother revealed to me. She started off explaining that she had in fact been in contact with Pop Pop even though her mother did not know. My mother explained that once she went away to school she was free to contact him without the worry of her mother finding out. However it wasn't the first time. Everyone summer while she was in high school she was in Panama and her mother thought she was spending it with her Aunt. Pop Pop's sister Yasmine, lived in Florida and stayed in touch with my grandmother even after she and Pop Pop split. Yasmine thought my mom deserved to be in her father's life so she didn't mind lying to my mother and sending my mom to Panama when she was supposed to be in Florida with her.

During the time she spent with Pop Pop the allure of the life he lived called her. It started with her doing minor things keeping books, sitting in on meetings, meeting new clients; but it quickly escalated. During her sophomore year of high school her brother, my uncle was murdered. Colon Panama is a pretty small place and in addition to that ever knew and respected Pop Pop. It didn't take long for him to get the names of those behind the hit. It was Los Jefes which at that time was run by Miguel's father. Of course my grandfather returned to panama with murder on his mind but not too far behind was my mother. She expressed that she had to be one the one to avenge her brother's death because although they lived apart he was everything to her. Pop Pop didn't like the idea but he knew in his heart that my mother could pull it off she he allowed it.

After weeks of planning her next move, she was ready. She boarded a flight to Mexico with one thing on her mind; blood. Ricardo was hard to get to but she didn't mind killing a few of his minions off to get to him. She knew having patience would pay off and it did in the best way. After killing Ricardo my mother said she returned home as if nothing happened. Finished high school and was off to Howard. While attending school at Howard mother ended up becoming a supplier to the DMV area, she could have expanded but didn't want to stray too far from her studies, which were still her main priority. She continued to visit my Pop Pop but they never spoke up the Ricardo, Los Jefes situation again.

As I looked at her confused. My mother, Ms. Goodie to shoes was a murder, and a drug dealer. I just couldn't wrap my head around that. She scolded me for the exact same things she had done. I couldn't even bare to look at her, I felt like the woman who gave birth to me was a stranger. I didn't know who she was. Laying in the hospital bed we gunshot wounds and a broken leg was the day my mother decided to introduce herself to me. I didn't want to hear anymore but she continued.

"That's when Hector..." She said before being cut off by my father who had now returned to the room.

"Don't you fucking dare Adriana." My father said while giving my mother a look that could have dropped her where she stood.

"Harvey, she told her everything. She might as well put it all on the table." Hector said, once again jumping to my mother's defense.

"He's right Harvey." My mother uttered before turning her attention back to me. She picked up where she left off, as my father stood in the corner shaking his head.

"I met Hector during the summers I visited…" She exclaimed.

I didn't know where she was headed but I knew it wasn't anywhere good.

"Mom please stop, I don't want to know any more. Please." I begged, hoping she would take heed and drop the subject altogether.

Surprisingly she digressed. She stepped back away from my bed and stood beside my father, who moved over putting a little distance between them. He thought I didn't notice it but I did. After the revelations she made I didn't have the energy to question anything else. I was ready for them all to go except Cameron. Just as I was going to speak up and let them know I didn't want the company any more, Hector moved closer standing in the spot my mother previously stood. He looked down at me and smiled. I had never paid attention to his facial expressions, or his features before because it wasn't necessary. However in that moment, I already knew. There was something familiar about him that reached beyond the months we have spent around each other.

"Skye, I'm your father." Hector declared, putting an end to all the speculation I had.

It felt like I had be stab in the chest repeatedly. I fought to catch my breath as I slowly slipped into hyperventilation. Hector reached down in attempt to calm me down but I quickly pushed his hands away. I didn't want him to touch me. They were liars! Each and every one of them lied to me in some way. I could have dealt with my mother having a secret life on the side but Hector being my dad was something I really couldn't wrap my head around. It's like my entire life as I knew was one big ass cover-up. I wasn't sure about anything at the point. Except for Cairo and Cameron. Cairo wasn't old enough to lie to me and Cameron, although he has been a jerk never was disloyal to me.

I looked over to him and he had the same expressionless face I had. He moved closer to me as to protect me and began to read my thoughts. No, I'm not psychic nor do Cameron and I share some sort of telepathic ability but I knew he knew what I was thinking. We were connected like that. He nodded his head to let me know he got me, and stood from his seat.

"Aight ya'll it's a lot for her to take in right now. So I'm saying everyone just dip and let her rest. Cairo and I will stay and if anything changes I'll definitely call." Cameron said in a serious tone.

They all looked over at me as if I was going to object but I wasn't. He spoke exactly what I was feeling. They needed to be gone, yesterday. Noticing that I wasn't going to go against what Cameron said, they each gave me an empty apology and left me alone with my boys.

Chapter Eighteen

Victoria

I lied in bed thanking god over and over for sparing all of our lives. Especially my baby and Cairo. They were innocent and didn't deserve to have to pay for the mistakes we made. I put my hand on top of Ty's which was resting on my protruding belly.

"Fuck!" I cried out as a sharp pain shot through my stomach.

"Babe you good?" Ty asked jumping up from his seat.

"I think something is wrong." I cried out as the pain hit me again. This time followed by a gush of water that flowed freely onto the bed beneath me. "No, not my baby." I cried while Ty got up to get a nurse.

Between the pain and the beeping of the machines I couldn't focus. All that played over and over was the nurse yelling out that I was in labor. I was only six months pregnant, it wasn't time. The baby was not ready. I couldn't comprehend why this was happening to me; moments ago they said everything was fine.

Ty held on to my hand until we reached the entrance of the Operating Room. He was stopped by the surgeon and denied access. I wished they would have allowed him to be in the room with me but I couldn't think about that too long. I needed to talk to god while I still had a chance. If it was anyone's time to go I prayed it was mine. Please spare my baby was what I kept repeating to god before I blacked out.

I woke up inside a hospital room, cold and alone. A single tear escaped my eyes as I tried to understand why Ty or my mother wasn't present with me. I felt my stomach; it was protruding but not like it was prior to me blacking out. Did my baby die? I thought fighting back tears. I felt around at my side before finding the button I was looking for. Moments later a nurse appeared at my side. I stared at her through squinted eyes. I was convinced in that moment that I was dreaming. It all had to be a nightmare.

"Ms. Carter, I'm glad you are awake." The nurse said smiling, showing me the deep dimples that were strategically placed on each side of her cheek.

"Where am I?" I asked.

I needed to know that this was all real.

"North Shore University Hospital." The nurse said giving me a concerned look.

It was real; I was indeed here alone, without my baby and she was indeed Ty's mother.

"My baby?" I asked frightened by the answer she would give me.

"He's in the NICU. Your mother and boyfriend is there with him. He's in good hands Ms. Lewis. Your doctor will be in shortly to give you official details of his status." She explained.

I sighed a bit of relief. I was aware that being born three months early put my baby at a lot of risk but he was alive. Wow, we had a boy. Ty and I wanted to be surprised about the sex but I was ecstatic finding out that we gave birth to a baby boy. Knowing that he was alive and Ty and my mother was with him really did put me at ease. There was another concern though. . The more she spoke her mannerism that Ty clearly inherited from her started to show. This was her there was no doubt in my mind. I remember her face from the picture, there's no way I could forget it!

"Excuse me." I said giving her a confused expression.

"Yes, what's wrong?" The nurse turned to me and asked.

I wanted to know, Ty deserved to know. Maybe it wasn't the right time.

"Oh never mind, everything is fine." I stated, concluding that we'll deal with it at another time.

"Okay sweetie I will be back to check on you in a bit." The nurse spoke turning to leave.

I couldn't just let her go. It was now or never!

"Erica?" I called out her name instantly getting her attention.

She looked at me through slanted eyes and gave me a half smile.

"Does he know Victoria?" She asked moving closer to my bed.

How did she know I knew? I shook my head no and saw her facial expression go from tensed to relax.

"He can't know. I'm supposed to be out of the country. I couldn't leave my baby boy behind although Jeff threatened to kill me if I didn't. I've looked after him from a distance his entire life. It killed me that I couldn't reach out to him but things were better with me out the picture." She started to explain.

"Jeff is dead." I said not allowing her to finish.

If Jeff is who was keeping her away from Ty all these years she no longer had that barrier in place. She was about to begin speaking when Ty walked into the room.

"Baby I'm so glad you're up. You should see him Vic, we had a son ma. My little man, he so tiny babe but he going to be Aight." Ty began speaking as soon as he got near my bed.

I held his hand and listened to him share the experience of seeing our son for the first time. He was unable to hold him but was able to touch his hands and feet through the holes in the incubator and that was good with him. Our son, who he kept calling TJ while he spoke, was alive and that's all that mattered. Whatever needed to be done in terms of his health would just be done. Erica stood back giving Ty and I space with a smile plastered on her face. She looked proud and I knew she was; her only son had just become a dad.

I listened to Ty talk about TJ and our future plans as a family until the medicine took over and I drifted off to sleep.

Skye

Cameron and I sat in silence while Cairo slept. I'm glad he didn't want to talk at that moment. He understood that I was trying to understand it all, I'm sure he was too. I was struggling to wrap my head around what was revealed to me. It was too much and Pop Pop was right. It wasn't the time nor was it the appropriate venue for them to drop those bombs on me. It just wasn't fair. I was lied to my entire life. What made matters worse was that they each had ample time to be honest. There was always an opportunity. Pop Pop should have told me about my mother and Miguel the minute he found out Miguel was the one who Cameron was being with. Instead, he convinced me to pay him. What's his end game?

I couldn't believe my mother. I knew it was something she was keeping from me from the reaction she gave when she saw Hector. That was her chance. She could have pulled me to the side and explained everything to me. Or when she was busy yelling and trying to scold me for taking over for Cameron. She could have said she was speaking from experience but no, she chose to lie. They all did.

My room door opened and my father, Harvey poked his head in. I didn't want to talk to him either. It was evident in my facial expression but that didn't stop him from coming in. Before I knew it he was staring beside my bed staring at me.

"Princess, I know that you don't want to be bothered right now but I need for you to hear me out." He stated.

I said nothing. I turned my head toward Cameron who took it upon himself to take Cairo from me and exited the room, leaving me, Harvey, and thick tension.

"Skye look at me please." My father spoke.

The hurt in his voice forced me to turn my head and look at him.

Once he was satisfied that he had my attention he started to explain himself again. Although I didn't want to listen I did. My father revealed to me that when my mother found out she was pregnant she was honest and told him that she had slept with Hector during a visit to Panama. He knew there was a possibility I wasn't his from the beginning but that didn't stop him from loving my mother or the child that was growing inside of her.

When I was born he and my mother flew out to Panama to talk with Hector who had no idea that my mother was pregnant. He was shocked but was willing to do what was in my best interest. He knew that there was no way he could just up and leave Panama and fly to the states to raise me and there was no way my mother was going to leave me there with him and Pop Pop. They came to the conclusion that it was best that my mother and Harvey stayed together and raised me. They all agreed not to get a DNA test because it made no sense, Harvey was my dad and that was it. It didn't stop Hector from sending money, or presents to the states for me. My father wasn't bothered by that at all. They had a mutual respect for each other. Until he found out that my mother got a paternity test done on me and Hector behind his back. Although he was pissed he still didn't get angry, he accepted the results for what they were and continued to raise me. That was the plan; he wasn't straying away from it.

My dad expressed that finding out Hector was in New York and thoroughly involved in my life is what pushed him to bury himself with work. Dealing with the fact that there was a possibility that I would find out Hector was my dad and allow him to come between us was too painful for my father. I understood that completely but what I didn't understand was how he could think that.

"You think that's all it takes from someone to replace you in my life dad?" I asked. He looked at me without saying a word so I continued. "Nothing or no one can replace you. You are the only father I know and have known my entire life. That can't be eradicated. You have been here for me in the worst of times. You have loved me unconditionally. Hector and I have been getting to know each other and I have grown to love him for what he has done for me lately. It still doesn't compare to the love I have you. I'm not upset about the situation things happen. I respect you for standing up and taking care of me without complaints even though you were aware that I wasn't your biological daughter. What hurts me is that you guys lied. You all didn't trust me enough with that truth and that really hurts dad." I spoke in a whisper.

"I'm sorry for the secrets, I'm sorry for the lies, and most of all I'm sorry for hurting you Skye. You are my world. I can't lose you." My dad said leaning down and kissing my forehead.

"You won't." I declared.

I didn't want to talk about it anymore so I asked him to go and get Cameron and Cairo. He was a little hesitant at first but eventually he did what I asked.

Chapter Nineteen

Pop Pop

I felt really bad leaving the hospital and leaving Skye to deal with our revelations on her own but I needed to set things in motion. I knew this day would come the moment I found out who Cameron was working for but I wanted to prolong it until Skye was out of harm's way which is why I convinced her to pay him the money. If she wasn't pregnant at the time things would have went totally different. There was no use on reflecting on how things would have been different it was time to move forward in rectifying the situation. My plans had to be changed and I had my men change their route and head to Mexico instead of coming to the states. Hector and I were going to be arriving shortly after. Since Miguel was roaming the streets of the United States I knew his home was under less protection as it would be if he was indeed there. I knew there would be guards but nothing that my men couldn't handle. Adriana insisted on going to Mexico with us but I needed her to tie up the loose ends in the stated when the time presented itself. It took us the entire ride to the airport for me to convince her that I knew what I was doing and my plan was fool proof. Hector and I promised to be in touch before boarding the plane for Mexico.

****

When we arrived we were greeted my three of my men would escort us to the safe house I had there. I made it my business to have property in every place I would potentially end up him for the exact reason I was there. Miguel wasn't one who stayed idle for too long so we had to move twice his speed. There was no time to waste, ever single minute wasted pushed us further away from being able to successfully complete the mission.

When we reached the safe house, my men were there and ready to fill me in on all the information they had gathered while staking out Miguel's estate and waiting for our arrival. Just as I expected, there was a small army of men guarding his house where his wife, three daughters, and mother was alone. Since I expected that, I was prepared for it. Like I usually am.

I delivered the orders, which were clear and concise. I wanted ever guard dead and the women brought to me at the safe house before sun rise. My men knew that if they let me down it would only mean death for them so I was sure they would deliver. After sending them on their way Hector and I got ourselves comfortable and prepared to wait.

****

As the sun peaked through the windows of the safe house, my men were pulling up with Miguel's family just as I asked. Each of the women were led into the house bound, gagged, and blind folded. I smiled at the handwork of my men as I took out my phone and called Adriana.

"Papa!" She spoke as she answered the phone.

"Go!" I said while I waited for her to proceed.

There was ringing coming from the call she added before Miguel answered.

"Who is this?" Miguel said as he answered the phone.

"Adriana." Adriana said putting on the thick Spanish accent she had picked up after all of the time she spent with me.

"Ahhh Adriiii, You must have found your daughter's body." He said letting out a laugh.

Adriana and I were both amused and returned his laughed.

"Well Miguel, I must say you inherited a lot from your father but lack his common sense." I said interrupting the gloating match that I was sure was going to take place between he and Adriana.

I walked over to Miguel's oldest daughter and slapped her before placing the phone to her hear and removing the cloth which muffled her sounds.

"Papi!" She screamed out into the phone.

I quickly hung up giving Adriana the lead way to complete things on her end. I looked back at Hector who sat quietly with the machete on his lap. I smirked as I approached him and lifted it up. Under normal circumstances his daughters would have been free to go, unfortunately for them there was nothing normal about the hell Miguel has caused my family.

I returned to where the five ladies were sitting and one by one beheaded them. Their heads rolled down their bodies and onto the floor. I handed the machete back to Hector.

"Clean this mess, package their heads and leave the boxes on Miguel's property. Hector get us a flight back to the states." I said before heading to my room to shower.

Adriana

After my father hung up the phone. I recited an address to Miguel and told him he had an Hour to show if he wanted to save his precious family. The address was one of the warehouses that Cameron told us they had access to in red hook. It was the perfect remote location for what I had planned.

I was sitting in the Security room of another one of Cameron's spots. This room had on going video footage of the various spots he had across the city. There was one screen I was watching intensely. When I graduated from Howard I thought I was going to put this life behind me for good. It was my intentions and I was doing a great job at sticking to it. However, once my daughter became heavily involved there was no way I could stand back and watch it happen. Especially when this all could have been avoided if I killed Miguel right along with his father. Ricardo was my first kill, and I was so nervous about getting away with it that I wasn't concerned about getting rid of his young son. If I would have known Miguel would grow to be a huge thorn in my child's life I would have. I couldn't cry over spilled milk all I could do was rectify the situation which I fully planned on doing.

My thoughts were interrupted as I watched four SUV's pull up to the warehouse. All the men jumped out with their guns drawn and ready to blast anyone who was there. Too bad they would be rushing into an empty space. I let out a hearty laugh as I watched Miguel exit the last truck and inter the building.

I waited a few minutes, to ensure that they were all inside and when I didn't see any more men exit one of the SUV's I proceeded with the plan. I hit the intercom button that was under the screen I was watching and began to speak.

"Welcome, please have your men put down their weapons Miguel." I spoke before hitting the next button to listen.

"Fuck you cunt bitch! Where is my family?" Miguel spat.

I smiled inwardly and pressed the intercom once again.

"I'm a woman of my word, you are going to see them right now." I said as I pressed the button on the detonator that was in my left hand.

I sat back and watched the building blow to pieces. The C4 that was strategically placed by Cameron's boys was enough to bring the entire building down. I watched as it went up flames and leaned back with a satisfactory smirk on my face.

Chapter Twenty

Ty

Vic was released from the hospital a week after she gave birth to TJ. Even though she wasn't a patient anymore we both were still residents between checking on Skye and staying with TJ from the start of visiting hours until they were over. Pop Pop, Hector, and Adriana handled the Mexicans. We didn't get many details on what went down but we didn't need the details. If they said it was handled then it was. All Cam and I had to do was focus on nursing the girls back to health and checking on TJ's progress. Doing that was nothing to us. Shit was actually going good until Aaliyah through a monkey wrench in and put Cam on game about Man planning on setting him up. I didn't trust shorty and even though she claimed she didn't want parts deep down I knew she was just as shady as her cousin.

Man was light weight so he wasn't really a priority in terms of us getting at him ASAP. We still controlled his blocks and he couldn't do shit about that unless he had the United States army behind him. He didn't, so that bitch ass nigga couldn't do nothing but keep calm until we brought the heat to him.

My main focus was my lil' nigga. TJ was getting stronger and stronger and I couldn't be happier about that. I was worried that my boy wouldn't make it but there he was nearly a month later and his progress was great. Little nigga was spoiled and had so much love around him. It's like the baby fever started spreading because shortly after all that shit went down Cam had slipped up and told me Skye was pregnant again. I didn't understand why it was a secret until he told me her doctor said the baby might not make. Skye was healing and her unborn seed was thriving shit was cool on the family front.

Vic ended up coming clean about her getting a private investigator to find my mom. Although I was pissed off with her from keeping that shit from me I knew her heart was in the right place. I didn't want to confront my mom at all nor did I want to hear what I felt like would have been a boat load of excuses but after talking it through with Vic and Mariah I decided maybe it wasn't such a bad idea. I surprised her at the hospital with flowers and offered to take her to lunch. Niggas couldn't tell me that she wasn't going to turn me down; but she didn't.

We kicked it at Olive Garden and she held no punches. According to her my father was married when she started fucking with him and when she found out she was pregnant and confronted him and his wife about it he said he wanted full custody and for her to disappear. Of course wasn't with that but that's when the death threats, and random ass whooping's started happening and she knew that the only way she would be able to keep her life was to give me to my father and his wife.

When I was just a few months old my father wife left him, which is why I have no recollection of the bitch what so ever. My mom's thought since she was out the picture my pops would let her back in my life but he didn't. The threats against her life continued and every time she showed up she left with bruises to show for it. Eventually she gave up but didn't leave the country like he told her to. She knew that one day she would be able to be in my life and didn't mind settling for watching over me from a distance if it meant that it would happen. She didn't expect it to take as many years as it did but she was happy that it happened. At first I thought her story was a bit shaky until the next few times we linked up and she showed me letters she had written to my dad asking to see me and the letters who wrote back cursing her out and threatening to kill her each time.

I was a dad and starting my own family, why not give my mom's the opportunity to be a part of TJ's life in ways she couldn't be there for me. If I was starting fresh I had to start completely fresh. Couldn't pick and choose. I ended up welcoming her into my life and so did the rest of the family. I even got to meet my little sister who is a mini me. The ringing of my cell phone brought me out of my own head.

"Yo." I answered without checking to see who was calling.

"Ty." My mother spoke bringing a smile to my face.

"Wassup ma?" I asked.

It was weird as fuck calling her ma but it made her smile and to be honest it felt good as shit to me.

"I was calling to check on TJ's progress. I know he's still progressing but it wouldn't feel right if I didn't check." She said sounding concerned.

"He good. Getting better and better every day." I said sounding like the proud father I was.

We kicked it for a minute about everything under the sun. That was something I had gotten used to. Moms was cool as fuck we could kick it about sports, music, video games, and of course the minor relationship problems I would have with Vic. Like I wanted her to be there my entire like she was finally able to be. It felt so right.

Skye

Since I been home from the hospital I had been spending a lot of time with my mother. Since everything that went down, when I found out about her ties to Pop Pop's organization I felt we needed to get to know each other for real. Just liked I always knew; we were no different. She did all the things she had done in her past to protect her family and those she cared about. Those were my exact reasons so how could I be mad at her. It didn't take me long to forgive her for that but getting over the fact that Hector was my father was a different hurdle.

One night while I was at Pop Pop's house in Staten Island I called my mom and dad over so that we could all sit down. In order for me to get over the situation I needed answers. Not the beat around the bush type answer but straight no chaser type answer. Although I spoke to my mom and dad separately and heard their separate versions of how it all went down, I needed them all together. The only way we were going to be able to move forward was together. Finally they granted me that. Whatever I asked they answered, no if's and's or but's were included. I learned that my mother and father were on a little break during the summer where my mother met and slept with Hector in Panama. When she found out she was pregnant with me she let them both know. She didn't want anything from Hector outside of the little time they spent together during the summer, and was planning a life with my dad, Harvey. The three of them agreed that a DNA test was not needed, and that Harvey would be the only father I ever known. Hector cared for me from a distance though. He sent money often which was never touched until I was given access to my account at eighteen. All the money I thought came from my parents was really from Hector. My mother ended up getting the DNA test done with just Hector because she didn't want to hurt my father's feelings. Her reason was because she knew it would come out one day and when it did she wanted to have definitive results to go. No maybes. I had already heard that all from my dad when we spoke while I was in the hospital. However getting the same facts from all three of them made it all better in a weird way.

I accepted hector into my life with ease because since I had met him he had been in my corner through it all, when he really didn't have to be. Harvey will always be my father no DNA result could ever change that. Now that everything was on the table he respected the relationship I wanted to have with Hector and Hector promised not to step on his toes.

Cameron and I were back together and our relationship had grown stronger than I ever. The Cameron I met and fell in love with was back one thousand percent and I couldn't be more proud of the man had he become due to the laundry list of peaks and valleys we had encountered. Neither of us was perfect but our flaws are what made us perfect for each other. Throughout everything we had been through I couldn't have seen myself going through it with anyone else. I just hoped that things stayed on this right path.

Chapter Twenty One

Ty

Cam and I were cruising through SOHO down Broadway. The plan was to hit up a few spots to get the women in our lives, Skye and Vic something special just to show them how much we appreciated them for holding us down through all the bull shit that's been going on. Wanted them to feel loved since they both had gone through some tough shit the past few months. TJ was home and doing well, and Skye was at a point in her pregnancy she didn't think she would reach. They deserved the world and more. I was getting ready to park when Cam tapped me on my shoulder to get my attention. I looked over at him and he pointed in the direction of the Prada store. I turned in the direction he was pointing and potted Man.

"What the fuck!" I exclaimed mad as hell; but nothing could compare to the look on Cam's face.

He looked like he was ready to kill that nigga right then and there. Cam's hand was on the door and he was about to hop out when I stopped him.

"Nah, Ty I'm not trynna here that bro you coming or not? I been waiting too long not to take this opportunity!" Cam shouted with a look of rage in his eyes.

I had to admit we had been waiting too long and that nigga Man just kept getting away somehow; but we couldn't just run up in the store and shoot the shit up that wasn't our style and never would it be.

"Look bro I know. Let's just wait till he come out though and follow him. Knowing that nigga he probably going to hide out at some bitch house." I said trying to reason with Cam.

Don't get me wrong I was ready to end that nigga life too but doing it in a public just wasn't a good idea. I could tell that Cam still wasn't sold on the idea of waiting from the look on his face and his tight grip on the door handle.

"Bro you not thinking this shit though its four of them nigga to two of us. What if something happens to me or you because you decided to just rush up in that bitch like swat and take matters into your own hands? What I'ma tell Skye and your mom's if you don't make it because I went along with this shit? Nigga, I ain't trynna let you die today and it definitely ain't my day to go either." I continued to plead my case.

I could tell from the words I just spit at Cam that he was starting to feel my idea a lot better. His tight ass grip on the door loosened and he turned in his sear looking straight ahead with his jaw tight.

"Aight Ty we gone do this your way but this nigga gotta die today. I'm tired of niggas thinking they can test me and get away with the shit." Cam replied.

I could tell from his words he was serious as hell and ready to get this shit done and over with. Let the games begin.

Cameron

At least forty five minutes had lapsed and that nigga was still in the store. You would have thought he spotted us and was hiding out. That wasn't likely though. I was getting antsy by the minute. I had so much rage built up for this nigga Man it wasn't even funny. If you could kill a nigga and kill them again I would do that to Man; no questions asked. I was about to say fuck it and just get out of the car and go alone and kill him if I had to. That's when I spotted Man and his crew coming out of the store with shopping bags. Ty looked over at me as he started the car back up.

"You ready to do this Cam?" Ty asked.

"Hell yeah bro." I said looking over at the truck that started moving with Man and his crew inside.

Ty knew I had been waiting for a while to catch this nigga man so I don't even know why he asked that question. As we took off following close but not to close behind Man and his crew. I couldn't help but think if I should let that bitch nigga die a slow death or just end it with a bullet to the head. Ty looked over and saw the small but present grin on my face.

"Tell me you thinking what I'm thinking." Ty stated.

I laughed because I already knew what my nigga was thinking without even having to question it.

"Yeah how we gone kill this nigga? I say let him die a slow painful death then shoot him." I retorted.

"I agree." Ty replied agreeing with me.

As we followed behind Man and them I noticed we ended up Brownsville. It was the hood, so I knew when we killed Man the boys wouldn't come right away. Reaching into the glove compartment I pulled out my nine and put the silencer on it. I took out the gloves that were tucked behind my nine and handed Ty a pair and slipped on a pair of my own.

Man had finally made it to his destination and hopped out of the car grabbing some bags. When his crew didn't I knew we was at one of Man's bitch's house or somebody crib who was close to him. This shit was going to be easier than I thought. We waited until the trucked pulled off to put our plain into motion. I watched intensely as Man knocked on the door. Shortly after he was greeted with a kiss by some chick neither me nor Ty knew. Nigga came to get ass, too bad it wouldn't get that far. Once they were both inside Ty and I jumped out the whip.

Deciding not to waste another minute Ty knocked on the door like it was nothing and he was expected. I had my nine aimed at the door not giving a fuck, ready to blast whoever opened it. The games were over. We played the cat and mouse game for too long with this nigga it was all coming to an end that day. When the door swung open I couldn't believe who it was, Aaliyah. She had a smile on her face but when she saw this shit wasn't a social call it faded instantly. She probably wouldn't have had any worries if she didn't lie to me. She talked a good game when she told me Man was trynna set me up. All that "I'm done with him Cam. I'm not fucking with him like that, family or not" shit was bull.

Ty and I both knew she was going to attempt to run but we couldn't have that. Ty quickly grabbed her and put his hand over her mouth to muffle her noises. Not even giving it a second thought I put a bullet right in the middle of her eyes, killing her instantly. Ty laid her on the carpet and closed the door.

Good thing I had the silencer on my piece, didn't want to alarm our target that we were on the scene. We followed Man's voice and the other bitch voice and led us into living room. I aimed my gun and pulled the trigger, causing the girls head to explode. No words needed to be shared. I wasn't there to give a speech nor did I want to listen to one. Man thought he was slick and tried to go for his gun, I halted that by letting off one hitting him in his kneecap.

"Ahhh shit!" Man screamed out grabbing his knee.

Was I supposed to feel guilty? Fuck no. I walked over to him and kicked him dead in the knee I just shot. I heard it crack and felt even better look on as he screamed out like a little bitch. Ty was laughing his ass off at that nigga.

"So tell me something Man. You thought you was gonna do all the shit you did and get away with it? I spat, not really giving a fuck if he answered the question or not.

Man just looked on with hate dancing around in his eyes. I expected more of a reaction, I needed more. It's been a long time coming and this nigga was trynna going out on some bitch shit. I drew back my hand and through a left hook that connected with his Jaw.

"Man up bitch!" I shouted watching as he grabbed his jaw. "Yo bro, go grab me a knife out the kitchen I got a surprise for this nigga." I stated.

Man eyes got big as shit once he realized how real it was about to get. I had to laugh because that nigga really was bitch made.

Man

There was a fiery throbbing sensation in my knee, shit hurt like hell. I watched as Ty handed the knife to that bitch ass nigga Cam. How the fuck did these niggas catch me slipping like this? I didn't know what he was about to do but I had to think quickly. I wasn't trying to give up without a fight. I tried to rise up off the couch and was stopped by another gun shot to my other knee.

"Fuck you son!" I screamed out in pain.

I felt tears come to my eyes because the pain was becoming unbearable. I wasn't ready to die but I knew that was Cam's end game. I just wished the nigga got it over with. My eyes widened as Cam raised the knife and slow began to slide it across the skin on my chest. I never been in so much pain in my life. I closed my eyes as he continued to inflict pain by making slashes across my chest. The blood began to flow from the cuts and I couldn't do a damn thing about it. When I did try to fight it I started to feel light headed.

"Cam, end it bro. Let's get low." I heard Ty say.

Cam shook his head up and down and stepped closer to me. Slowly he started to slit my throat. I reached up and grabbed my throat and felt the blood ooze from it. I couldn't scream or do shit. I was dying slowly and painfully. I prayed the nigga would just end it. After watching the life leave my body for a few minutes he finally decided it was time. I watched Cam raise the gun till it leveled with my head. I closed my eyes and began to ask God to forgive me for all the shit I've ever done.

Cameron

I pulled the trigger and watched the bullet enter his skull, and his lifeless body slumped over. Man was the last piece of the ongoing string of bullshit that has be occurring in my life this past year. It was finally over. I looked over at Ty who confirmed that he was thinking the exact same thing I was thinking and all he had to do was nod his head.

We didn't waste any more time lingering around and left undetected. During the ride back to my crib we kicked it about everything that had transpired since I met Skye. We made it, and really couldn't understand why. The life we lived only guaranteed two exit options, cuffs or a coffin. Yet there we were free and alive. We both knew it was time to get shit right. We were family men. Ty had Vic and TJ, I had Skye, Cairo and our baby girl on the way who we decided we would name Faith. Thinking about where we started and how we have grown brought me to the realization that we needed to be over this shit. It wasn't a necessity anymore. My dad wasn't here so I had nothing to prove to him, my family had bread that would last longer than I would probably live so that wasn't an issue either. There was nothing keeping either of us in the game and the more we spoke about it out loud the more realized it.

As we pulled up to the crib we made a vow to each other that the Man situation was it. We were putting the past in the past and looking at a much brighter future. I knew what my next step would be and with Skye's birthday coming up I knew exactly when I was going to take it.

Chapter Twenty Two

Skye

I walked into Rose Castle and was bombarded with a giant surprise. I told Cameron and my parents that I didn't want a party but of course they didn't listen. I felt like a whale and was always ready for a nap. Who could possibly enjoy a party in those conditions? I didn't want them to feel bad about their surprise so I put on my poker face and greeted each happy birthday I received with a thank you and a smile.

"Baby, you like?" Cameron said running up behind me and placing his hands on my stomach.

"I do. Babe you really didn't have to go through all of this I was totally fine with a nice intimate dinner with just the family." I said turning to face him so that he could give me a kiss.

I puckered my lips to him and he leaned over and placed his succulent lips on mine.

"I know that Skye, but you deserve this. I love you."
He said before Victoria approached us giving him the chance
to get away.

"Happy Birthday old lady!" Victoria said pulling me
in for a hug.

"Thanks Vic, Where is my baby? I see bad ass Cairo
running around he usually attached to whoever has TJ." I
said while laughing.

"He was girl, mom is over there with him but he fell
asleep. Soon as he was knocked out Cairo dipped on her."
Victoria said join me in laughter.

I had to admit that although I didn't want a party it
was turning out to be a great evening. It has been so long
since everyone could get together and party like we had no
worries and it felt good having that opportunity. It was nice
to see both my dad's and mom there getting along. Pop Pop
had returned as well so he wouldn't miss it. Everyone who
was near and dear to me was present, which included the
select few of Cameron and Ty's homeboys that we
considered family.

The night was amazing and I honestly didn't think it
could have gotten any better. I should have known though
when it came to Cameron.

"Attention!" Cameron shouted while standing on the
stage in the middle of the room with a mic in his hand.

My eyes locked with his and he motioned for me to join him on the stage. I really didn't want to get up from the seat I was in because my feet where killing me. I also didn't want to ruin whatever it was he had planned so I got my fat butt up and wobbled over to the stage. He took my hand and helped me up the steps before continuing to address the guest.

"First off I want to thank you all for coming out and celebrating my baby birthday with us. I could never really thank you all enough for making this a night she really deserved." Cameron turned to me and kissed me on my forehead.

"Skye from the day you bumped into me I knew you were the woman I would spend the rest of my life with. Real shit, everything about you screamed forever. You're intelligent, hella beautiful, driven, and sassy as shit. I can't forget that you're definitely a rider. I couldn't have picked a better woman to share my life with, let alone bare my children. I appreciate you and everything that encompasses you. I love you with every fiber of my being and I know this type of love will never die. I'm content and extremely happy with the way things are now but I know it could get better. In order for that to happen we gotta do it right." Cameron stated before retrieving a small ring box and dropping down to one knee.

He opened the ring box and my eyes fell on the most beautiful Princess Cut Canary ring. A smile spread across my face as he continued to speak.

"So here, in front of all our family and friends. I'm hoping that you don't embarrass a nigga and turn me down." Everyone laughed.

"Nah, but seriously Skye. Let's do it right. For Cairo, for Faith, and the true love that we share. Will you marry me?" Cameron asked with a grin wide as the equator.

It took a minute for me to respond. Not because I was thinking about my answer but because I was taking in the moment. I looked to my right and saw my mom and Mariah both wiping the tears away that escaped during Cameron's proposal then I turned back to him.

"Of course I will Cameron. I love you so much!" I shouted as he stood to his feet and pulled me in for a kiss.

The entire hall erupted into cheers, and people were shouting congrats left and right. As I stood in his embrace I quickly reflected on everything that led up to that moment, whether it be good or bad. It was worth it.

Chapter Twenty Three
(8 Months Later)

Cameron

"I recalled when we first met, a long time ago. How could I forget the way I felt, when I first laid eyes on you? I remember saying to my friends, there is my future wife; and then, I took the steps to meet someone who would change my life." Gerald Levert's smooth baritone voice began to sing as the tune of "Made to love you" began to play signaling that it was finally the moment I've been waiting for since the day I met her. I looked straight ahead holding my breath. Finally I was able to breathe when I saw the love of my life appear at the top of the flower filled walkway. She was accompanied by both of her fathers. Harvey and Hector both wore a smile on their face bright enough to light the darkest room. They made slow strides down the aisle while Luther's voice serenaded the crowd filled with those closest to us.

"I have everything I ever wanted." I thought to myself looking over to where Adriana sat holding my baby girl Faith, right beside her was my Prince, Cairo. He sat

swinging his legs staring intensely at his mom as she made her way toward me. Everything we been through leading up to that moment was all worth it if this was the outcome. I only planned on doing the marriage thing once and a nigga was proud as hell that it was with Skye.

When she finally came to a stop in front of me I reached out and held her hands in mine.

Skye

Feeling his touch still gave me butterflies. Standing before preparing to take vows in front of god, our family, and friends was a surreal moment. Who would have thought after all the trials our relationship had endured we would make it to this moment. I was the little girl who dreamed of a huge fairytale type wedding and it was all there, I was marrying my soul mate, and we had two beautiful children. Having Cairo and Faith really solidified Cameron and my relationship. Our children bought out the best in us and had us wanting to do right for them and for ourselves. I had them to thank for this moment.

I thought about the life Cameron and I planned to have with the kids as the preacher began the Ceremony.

"Dearly beloved, we are gathered here today, on this very happy and joyous occasion, to join Cameron and Skye in holy matrimony. Marriage is a solemn institution to be held in honor by all, it is the cornerstone of the family. It requires of those who undertake it a complete and unreserved giving of one's self. It is not to be entered into lightly, as marriage is a sincere and mutual commitment to love one another. This commitment symbolizes the intimate sharing of two lives and still enhances the individuality of each of you." He pronounced.

As he spoke I couldn't help but to imagine the future Cameron and I would have with our children. My babies meant the world and more to and I couldn't thank Cameron enough for assisting me in bringing them into the world. My life was finally how I saw it. It was really happening, I felt a rush of blood which felt as if it was forming puddles in my cheek and I knew I was blushing. Thank goodness my face was still hidden behind the veil.

"Cameron, do you take Skye to be your wedded wife? Do you promise to love her, comfort her, honor and keep her in sickness and in health, remaining faithful to her as long as you both shall live?" The pastor said bringing to my attention that this was indeed the moment that dreams were made of.

I looked at Cameron as he began to move his succulent lips. I couldn't wait to kiss them once again. We have been separated for three whole days and I was yearning for a kiss from my love.

"I do!" Cameron shouted causing a low giggle to flow through the crowd.

He was anxious and it was obvious. I couldn't front, I was too. There we were, one step away from be Mr. and Mrs. Carter. Surreal was an understatement in terms of how I felt about that moment. Nonetheless I was extremely happy and felt extremely blessed.

"Skye, do you take Cameron to be your wedded husband? Do you promise to love him, comfort him, honor and keep him in sickness and in health, remaining faithful to him as long as you both shall live?" The pastor said turning his attention to me.

I felt like jumping up and down and screaming of course. However, I knew I needed to contain my excitement. At least for a few more minutes.

"I do." I said fighting back the urge to cry.

There were a few more word delivered by the pastor and before I knew it I was in Cameron's arms. On the receiving end of the most passionate kiss we have ever shared. I don't know if it was because I'd been wanting it for three long days or because it was just that intense. A mixture of both I suppose.

The crowd of our guest erupted in applause as I intertwined my arm with Cameron's and jumped the broom. Not lasting any more than an hour my ceremony was everything I dreamt it being and more. Departing the area where my ceremony was held, was when I had the chance to really bask in the beauty of the venue. Cipriani was very sophisticated. It was set in an Italian Renaissance theme; with towering columns, a soaring ceiling, and gorgeous inlaid floors. It was everything I dreamed of since I was a young girl.

We were led to the area where our reception was being held and shared our first dance. Mariah Carey and Luther Vandross's "Endless Love" boomed throughout the room as my husband and I danced. I was so focused on him everyone else in the room became invisible. I was on a cloud, one that I never wanted to come down from.

"I love you Mrs. Carter." Cameron whispered in my ear before twirling me into the arms of my father. It was time for the father daughter dance.

"I love you more Mr. Carter." I yelled above Beyoncé's "Daddy."

I shared the dance between both of my fathers and neither of them seemed to mind. It probably was a bit unorthodox but I couldn't say that I would have rather had it any other way. Girls were lucky and blessed to have one father, I was beyond that. I had two who loved me dearly and that made the moment all that more special.

The sentimental moments were coming to an end and the reception was underway. I held faith in my arms while we danced with the two most important men in our life; Cairo and Cameron. Things were going great and everyone was having an amazing time. I was all smiles until a dark gloomy feeling came over.

Taking notice Cameron pulled me to the side to inquire about my change in mood.

"Baby what's wrong?" He said looking extremely concerned.

"I don't know Cameron. I just had this feeling come over me. Something isn't right." I stated staring deep into his eyes.

Faith was squirming in my arms so I bounced her gently to calm her down. That worked like a charm.

"Baby everything is perfect. Look around." He said flashing me a reassuring smile.

I took his advice and scanned the room of our loved ones. That's when I spotted what wasn't right. I was too late. All I remember was gun fire erupting and catastrophe taking place. Cameron pulled Cairo, Faith and I into the corner and ran toward the pandemonium while retrieving two colts from the inside of his tuxedo jacket.

"Noooo Cameron!" I screamed out over the gunfire.

Faith was now throwing a fit of piercing screams, which trickled down to Cairo as well. Cairo was crouched down in the corner with his hands over his ears calling his dad over and over. As bad as I wanted to run after Cameron my children where the priority. I pulled them close to me used my body as a shield. It brought back memories of when I was shot but I shook my thoughts off. The gun fire seemed to be never ending. All I could think about was how the best day of my life turned into a giant nightmare.

After what seemed like forever the gun fire had finally ceased. All that could be heard was screams. I was afraid to move. Not for me but because of my babies. Although the gun fire had stopped I hadn't had a clue if it would start again. I couldn't risk it.

"Come on sis." Ty said as he reached us.

He helped me up from the crouching position I was in and took faith out of my arms.

"I'm not leaving Cameron." I cried.

"He will be fine Skye please trust me and let's go." Skye barked.

I hesitated for a second before grabbing Cairo and following behind Ty. Once we were outside Ty led us to the limo where Victoria and TJ were and opened the door.

"Get in, ya'll leaving." He said.

I looked from the limo back to Cipriani and back to the limo again. I kissed Cairo and ushered him into the limo before pecking Faith on her forehead and running back into the building.

Cameron

This shit was out of control. *I knew these Mexican motherfuckers would try to retaliate for Miguel's death but why did it have to be today?* I thought as assessed the scene. I was looking for my wife and my kids, my mother too. I really just needed to see that my son and daughter was straight. Amongst the cold bodies were a bunch of dead Mexicans. Good for their bitch asses I thought to myself as I continued to look. None belonged to any of my family so I was straight. I spoke entirely too fast. As soon as I hit the corner I walked up on a scene I wish I could have went back in time to correct.

I walked closer not believing that this was real when I heard my name called.

"Cameron!" I turned to see Skye quickly approaching me.

I was screaming for her to stop and turn around but the words weren't coming out. I was in shock. She got closer, and I looked down at the scene before me and back to her. *Don't come over here baby.* I was silently thinking. I couldn't verbalize the words for shit. I was too late.

The moment she walked up near me and got a better look at what I saw, she fell to her knees and let out a gut wrenching scream.

"Mommmmy!" She screamed out as she crawled over to where. Adriana lied motionless in the arms of Harvey.

Pop Pop was beside Harvey on the floor applying pressure to her wombs. In attempt to stop the bleeding. It was impossible, there was blood running from a hole in her chest and one on the side of her head. Her eyes were open and they were lifeless.

"Mommy please, get up! I need you mom please. Cai and Faith needs you." Skye cried leaned over and pulling Adriana closer to her.

I bent down and attempted to pick her up to take her away but she swung violently and continued to scream. Sirens could be heard and I was carrying, leaving Skye wasn't an option so I took off my Tux jacket and held the gun as I wiped the prints with my shirt. Still holding them with my jacket I put them down and kicked them away from me. My attempts to remove Skye from Adriana's body were useless. It pained me in a way I couldn't explain to watch Skye breakdown. I knew the feeling all too well since I too had lost a parent. I wouldn't have wished that pain on a random ass person so it killed me watching Skye go through it.

Police arrived on the scene as well as paramedics, and that's when we were finally able to separate Skye from Adriana.

"No, let me go!" Skye screamed and kicked trying to break free from my grasp.

I pulled her closer, and tightened the grip I had on her. She sank into my chest and sobbed.

"Why my mom?" Skye cried as I rubbed her back.

"I'm sorry baby, I really am. I got you though Skye, you're not alone. We will get through this together." I said. It didn't matter how genuine I was. Nothing I said would heal her pain or fill the void. It would take a while, but I had intentions on holding her hand the entire way.

Skye

The burial was over and I watched everyone take slow strides to their cars. I wouldn't move. I couldn't even if I wanted to. This was my last chance to say goodbye to my mother and I was still unable to believe that it really was happening. She was supposed to be here to help me with Cairo and Faith. She was supposed to be here for me to cry on her shoulder when Cameron and I went through our issues. She was never supposed to leave me.

"Why did you leave me mommy?" I inquired as I fell to my knees and sobbed before her plot.

I didn't care that I was in a dress, on my knees in the dirt. My mother was gone. There would be no more girls days spent shopping and going to the Spa. No more girl talk. Nothing! All I was left with was memories. I wanted, and needed more. I looked up and spotted Cameron walking toward me. He had left my side for a minute just to take

Cairo and faith to the limo. He was stopped by Hector. After the two shared a few words Hector walked away from Cameron and headed in my direction. Cameron didn't move though, he stood there looking at me ready to rush to my side need be.

I was engulfed in sobbing and saying out loud that I wish it was all a nightmare and that I would wake up any minute when I felt Hectors arm go around my shoulder as he fell on his knees and pulled me close to him.

"Let it out Skye." Hector said as he rubbed my back.

I sobbed into his shoulder and asked why my mother left me over and over.

"She is everything to me Hector. Why? I'm alone now. It wasn't supposed to be like this. It's my fault. I should have listened when she told me not to pursue handling Cameron's business she would be here if I didn't. My mom is gone." I cried out.

"This is in no way your fault Skye. You are not alone Skye. You have Cam, you have you beautiful children, your grandfather, Harvey, and you have me. You are surrounded by so many people who love you. We will help you through this. You don't have to try to be strong for everyone anymore. It's our turn to be strong for you and we will." Hector tried to assure me.

"Dad is so out of tune with everything. I need to be there for him and help him. Pop Pop already made plans to leave and I know you will be leaving too. Everything is so messed up."

"Your father needs time. Just like you he is hurting and trying to cope with the loss of his wife. We are here for him too believe me. Harvey and I don't always see eye to eye but I got love for him too he's raised you. How could I not. Your grandfather is leaving because he has to. I on the other hand will not leave you. Not like this. I haven't been here for a lot of things but this I will definitely see you through. Don't worry about that." Hector said as he helped me up.

Cameron saw that Hector helped me up and scurried to my side. I through myself into his arm and he squeezed me. Letting me know that he had me. He scooped me into his arms and carried me towards our Limo. I looked over his shoulder and whispered goodbye to my mom. I knew that it wouldn't be an easy journey but at the same time I knew the best thing for myself and those around me was for me to start looking toward the future.

Epilogue

Since the death of her mother Skye had become a completely different person. She wasn't cold or frigid as you would expect someone to be after suffering such a great loss. Her view on life was different. She felt as if losing her mother was the ultimately price she had to pay for all the wrong she had done. It was also her chance for the fresh start she always voiced that she wanted. Finding her way back to church after many years of not attending a service her healing journey had begun. She was no longer interested in anything related to the street, her only interest were being the best mother she could be to Cairo and Faith. She completed her studies and earned her Juris Doctor Degree, which was the first step to taking over and successfully running her mother's Law Firm. She isn't where she would like to be emotionally, but she's getting there. It wasn't a journey she had to endure alone, there was the constant help of her father, her grandfather, and the love of her life. Although Pop Pop returned to Panama he made it a priority to stay involved in the lives of Skye, and her kids. Hector kept his promise and stayed behind, although he takes frequent tips back home.

As promised Cameron kept his word to Skye and refrained from running the street. After all the losses they suffered and sacrifices they have made collectively. He finally arrived at the realization that none of it was worth it. He had his children, his wife, and more than enough money to last them a lifetime. He too had completed school and possessed a Juris Doctor degree. He ended up getting a Job offer working at Harvey's sports agent firm where he is now a partner. In his spare time he picked up the niche of writing and penned a few titles based on the he and Skye's life. In addition to work he is focused on being a loving and doting father to his children as well as a husband to Skye.

Since TJ is a little older Victoria finally kept her promise to Skye and went to school. She got a degree in nursing and has started working at Miami University Hospital under Skye's grandparents. She and Ty moved back there shortly after their wedding to give TJ the taste of a different life besides city life. Victoria was pretty content with her new life but the allure of the street calling her was a battle she fought every day. You know what they say old habits die hard.

Ty's chance to be the boss finally presented itself. He didn't need to cross his longtime friend to get there either. With Cameron completely out of the game his empire was up for grabs. Who else would be better suited than the one who was there from the start? However, after the dust had settled even Ty wanted more. After moving back to Miami, he decided to go into business with Pop Pop. Legit business! They ended up opening a Club and restaurant right in south beach. His relationship with his mother had evolved tremendously and eventually she and his little sister joined Ty and Victoria in Miami. Even though Ty felt having his wife, son, and in-laws was the only family he really needed, at the end of the day he finally felt complete once Erica and his sister entered his life.

Pop Pop had the business in Miami with Ty but he still had an organization to run. He returned to Panama a few months after Adriana's death to resume his business. He visits often enough to touch bases with Ty and spend time with Skye and her kids. For Hector going back to Panama wasn't an option. Although he still respected the relationship Skye had with Harvey he still didn't want to leave her. The secret was out so he planned on being 100% active in her life. There was money to be in the states and with Cam and Ty out of business leaving a team of money hungry young boys to fend for themselves, Hector picked up the slack. So essentially it was business as usual for him he just got a chance to be near his daughter and grandkids.

The crew learned the hard way that everyone has an agenda whether it be good or bad. Everyone wants to be in some position of power. There's nothing wrong with that. It's what you do to achieve your position that defines you as a person.

Acknowledgements

Wow, three books down! I can't put into words how extremely blessed I am for being provided such an opportunity. I must thank god first and foremost for the continuous blessings he bestows upon me.

Mommy and Grandma life wouldn't be life without ya'll. I love you both to the moon and back.

My family and friends who have supported me on this journey I appreciate you.

Nyeema, Promise, Janelle, Kiki, Chanel, Ariel, Tipzy

To the loyal readers who have been on this Power Trip with me from part 1 this book would not have blossomed into what it is if it were not for you guys. Thank you.

Shawnda, Kyra, Brittaknee, Gina, Erinn, Mariser, Cleopatra, Vanessa, Gabriela, Susan, Pookie, Jane, Melissa, Sandra, Tonya, Tenita, Ceardra, Alaina, Lashonda, Crystal, Jaquita, Victoria Jackson

Authors who support me; Love is Love.

Mercedes Taylor, Christine, Anjela, Yara, Naporcha Dion, CoCo J, Danielle Grant, Jasmine Barber, Boo Jackson, Helen, Neeka, Teeka, Wallace, Ivory B, Bella Jones... It's so many more of you guys, I'm so sorry if I forgot you. Just know that I thank you and I support you as well.

My extended Reading/Writing family <3

Demettrea, Alisha, Charmanie, Mia, Mika, Angelique, Yanni. I don't know where to start. We've shared some late nights and early mornings discussing everything from books to politics. Having writing sessions, or just kicking it. I'm glad I've had the chance to meet you ladies. Love ya'll to bits and wish ya'll nothing but success in all of your endeavors.

#PPP Thanks for the opportunity.

Raymond Francis & Envy Seal

If I didn't mention you please know it doesn't mean you are appreciated any less.

CPSIA information can be obtained
at www.ICGtesting.com
Printed in the USA
LVHW040329040919
629883LV00026B/2864/P

9 781493 785810